**Praise for TRAC...**

W9-DDQ-157

★ "The beauty of this rigorously unsentimental novel about a family in crisis is the way that Mack, even as she lets her characters' imaginations soar, keeps her story grounded in the pain of broken things. . . . The words remain powerfully ambiguous, the healing poignantly attenuated."

—*Booklist*, starred review

★ "The setting is the star in this moving portrayal of a boy coming to terms with his brother's death set in New York's East Village. . . . Loss, compassion, and forgiveness are primary themes, realistically and sometimes painfully drawn through the interactions of Joseph's family. . . . [A] remarkable work."

—*Kirkus Reviews*, starred review

"Ma... ...try realistically
capt... ...and the possi-
ble... ...tory's painful
sens...

—*...ibrary Journal*

"Mack... ...weirdness of
New Y... ...d loss and is
search... ...ingly real. A
lovely...

—*KLIATT*

"*Birdlan...* ...ike familiar
chords... ...rks his way
through...

—...ean Myers

"Stealing... ...cy Mack's
novel *Bi...* ...ves back a
breathta...

—...Osborne

...ank Street College Best Book

## For the Best in Literature

**POINT**

*Fallen Angels*
**Walter Dean Myers**

*From the Notebooks of Melanin Sun*
**Jacqueline Woodson**

*Learning to Swim*
**Ann Turner**

*Make Lemonade*
**Virginia Euwer Wolff**

*My Brother Sam is Dead*
**James Lincoln Collier and Christopher Collier**

*Plain City*
**Virginia Hamilton**

*Slam!*
**Walter Dean Myers**

*Toning the Sweep*
**Angela Johnson**

*When She Hollers*
**Cynthia Voigt**

*When She Was Good*
**Norma Fox Mazer**

*Winter*
**John Marsden**

# BIRDLAND

# TRACY MACK

## PO/NT

SCHOLASTIC INC.

New York  Toronto  London  Auckland  Sydney
Mexico City  New Delhi  Hong Kong  Buenos Aires

No part of this work may be reproduced, stored in a retrieval system, or transmitted in any form or by any means, electronic, mechanical, photocopying, recording, or otherwise, without written permission of the publisher. For information regarding permission, write to Scholastic Inc., Attention: Permissions Department, 557 Broadway, New York, NY 10012.

ISBN 0-439-53591-3

12 11 10 9 8 7 6 5 4 3 2                                        5 6 7 8 9/0

Printed in the U.S.A.                                                      40

First paperback printing, December 2004

Grateful acknowledgment is made for permission to reprint excerpts from *Our House: The Stories of Levittown* by Pam Conrad, copyright © 1995 by Pam Conrad. Reprinted by permission of Scholastic Inc.

The text type was set in Perpetua and Quartet small caps. The display type was set in Motherlode loaded AOE and Squarehouse solid.
Photographs © 2003 by Marc Tauss ★ Book design by Marijka Kostiw.

This book is a work of fiction. It is not authorized by or affiliated with the estate of Charlie Parker, his music publisher, or anyone affiliated with them.

ART COMPLETES

WHAT NATURE

CANNOT BRING

TO FINISH. — ARISTOTLE

# "BONGO BOP"

Flyer and me, we're down here in the basement of New York City. Jamal is drumming, grinning. Sweat beads around his hairline. Sound bounces off the white tile walls and over the subway tracks. It gets the attention of a few souls. Most are reading, talking, or doing the head-dip over the rails, as if that's going to speed up the train.

"Yeah, man." Flyer cranks his wrist at Jamal and tosses a dollar into his upturned hat. It joins a pile of coins. Hardly enough for two slices of pizza.

Flyer's new machine, cradled in my right fist, is the Ferrari of video cameras. I zoom in and shoot Jamal.

HIS HANDS ARE LIKE PING-PONG PADDLES.
HIS VOICE IS LIKE WIND CHIMES.

1

Every few beats the song sails in, not words but sounds, full up with feeling. I want to shout out my appreciation, but instead I just pump my left fist in the air. In my head, words do their usual dance, lining up and moving forward, then crashing at the door. They are all wrong coming out.

Flyer doesn't ask many questions. He is my best bud.

I turn and shoot him, rocking his tall, twiggy body, which is curved like a question mark. He has spiky dyed hair, cloud-colored. A galaxy of rings up his left ear. His skateboard always. I gave him the name Flyer for the way he moves on wheels.

Flyer is what you'd call a floater. He can drift in and out of any group at school — hippies, punks, Goths, brains, prepsters, artists, even the jocks. Used to be I could slide in on Flyer's recommendation. But that was before this year, before everyone started looking at me like I'm damaged goods.

A drunk guy staggers into my field, red-eyed

and swearing. His right arm flails like a piece of trash in the wind. He's not your typical drunk. He's wearing a suit and tie that look like he's been sleeping in them for the past week. Even from ten feet away he stinks. "Yer all a buncha ingrates, you are. This man's a genius, agenuinegeniushere, can'tcha see?"

"You know what I'm sayin'," Flyer echoes the sentiment.

Jamal flashes a grin.

The drunk guy stumbles over and drapes an arm around him and starts to dance. Jamal keeps on drumming. He doesn't break his rhythm or his smile.

The drunk guy is practically hugging him as he sways and croons some tuneless song. He does this for several minutes, and I just keep shooting. Velly told us to look for colorful material.

Then, before I know it, the drunk guy is shouting, "Hey, son! Yer suppos'ta ask someone's permission before you film them. I could sue you for privacy infringement."

Privacy infringement? My father, Dr. Bob, is not only an obstetrician but a nonpracticing New York State attorney. I've been listening to him spout off legal jargon for as long as I can remember, and I've never heard of anything called privacy infringement.

I'm so fixated on the bogus term that it takes me a few beats to realize the guy is coming toward me. I move the camera away from my face and try to tell him that he walked into my shot. Only it comes out all slow, as usual, like I've got a spoonful of glue in my mouth.

"Hey, you makin' fun a me, son?" He stumbles closer.

"Easy, man." Flyer takes him by the arm.

"Don't touch me, son. That's called assault in a court of law." He's spraying saliva all over Flyer's face.

Flyer lets go and wipes his face with the back of his hand. "Just leave my friend alone, dude. He's not breaking any laws."

"Oh, yeah, he needs a film release unless he plans to give me the tape." He lunges toward me.

I should be scared, I guess, because my right foot is just inches from the edge of the platform and one swift shove could make me fried calamari on the third rail. But all I can do is marvel at this man's abilities to string sentences together when he looks like he might pass out any second.

Flyer throws his body between us and presses his fingers into the man's chest.

I don't even realize that the music has stopped until I see Jamal's broad body behind the drunk. Jamal takes him gently by the shoulders. "Easy, soldier. These brothers are just makin' a little video for school. No need to get physical."

The drunk guy mumbles a few words I can't understand. Is that how I sound?

5

Jamal steers him to a row of wooden seats and parks him. A few people have tuned in to the drama. They go back to their books and conversations as the man settles down.

Jamal pats his shoulder. "Easy now, soldier."

When Jamal turns back to his drum, we follow. He leans down to pick up a bottle of apple juice, swigs and swallows. Flyer presses his hands into prayer position and gives him a grateful nod. I take Jamal's free hand and squeeze it.

"You brothers be smart," he says. "New York City ain't no place to be careless."

The word *careless* hangs in the air for a moment, like the drunk guy's stench. Then Jamal sets down his juice and taps out a song so mellow, I never knew such a sweet sound could come from a drum.

# "STREET BEAT" TWO

We're on the street now. I sweep the camera and scan the avenue. I pull back to get a wide beauty of a shot.

According to this book on documentary film-making that I checked out of the school library, it's important to establish your setting first. I've watched a few documentaries, one on skateboarding that Flyer and I went to see together and some that his mom made, on things like teen dads and queer youth. Plus, my dad's got a whole library of documentaries by this guy Ken Burns.

We're getting footage for an assignment that our English teacher, Mr. Velasquez, gave us over winter break. He asked us to record our neighborhoods. We had just finished reading a book called *Our House,* by Pam Conrad, which is about six kids growing up in the same suburban neighborhood over six decades. Even though my East Village neighborhood covers a few blocks in New York City and is nothing like the burbs, Ms. Conrad had a way of making you feel like the book was about you.

Velly read the end aloud before we left on Friday:

> *Keep in mind that you are making memories.*
>
> *Consider that something you take for granted today may be the one thing you might pine for someday, and there might not be any more of it left, but you'll remember its sweetness. Remember the curve of the sun in your bedroom window late in the day, the way your little brother's hair smelled after his bath, and*

*the sound of your mother and father talking in*
*the kitchen.*

*Make sure you notice if the trees meet in*
*an arch over your street, or if there's a certain*
*sound that you hear at a particular time every*
*day. Take note of those people who are so famil-*
*iar to you, and consider memorizing them for a*
*time when they are gone.*

*And know that if anyone ever says to you,*
*"What will you always remember about this*
*place?" you will know just exactly which story*
*it is that you would tell them.*

Velly's voice cracked on that last part, which
made Jackson Dumas and a few other jerks in
the back of class laugh. Normally Velly would
call a dude out on such a thing, but he must
have been pretty caught up in the words he'd
just read because he let it slide. He told us

that Ms. Conrad had died shortly after she'd written the book, which made the words kind of haunting.

Velly cleared his throat and told us that for the assignment, we could write, paint, sing, or create any other expression we could think of. He said that this would give us a chance to portray our neighborhoods as we saw them. And because kids at our school come from all over Manhattan and the boroughs, when we put it all together in January, our class's work will form a city collage. He also said that, symbolically, creating something was one way to rebuild the pieces of our damaged city and repair our broken hearts. "True healing," he said, "begins with imagination."

Mr. Velasquez is a smart guy, but I'm not sure about what he said. So what if you *imagine* something to be healed. It's still the same broken thing, isn't it?

On the bright side, Flyer's got this new pricey video camera from his mom, all the way from San Francisco. She and his dad split up over the summer, and she moved out there. What Flyer really wanted was for his mom to come back and work things out with his dad. But as far as presents go, the camera is an amazing machine.

As soon as Velly announced the assignment, Flyer signaled to me that we should use it. Velly also said you could work with a partner if you lived in the same neighborhood, and without even talking about it, Flyer and I knew we'd collaborate. We've been inseparable *compadres* since we met back in fifth grade.

Before we left for our ten-day vacay, Velly said, "Take it seriously, *amigos*. *Enséñame un mundo nuevo*. Show me a new world." His hands were flying. His eyes shining. "Show me magic, *amigos*!"

You've got to love the guy.

If you ask me, there aren't too many people in the world who care half as much as Velly. His enthusiasm and the fact that I'm looking for something — anything — to get me through the holidays have me into making this neighborhood documentary.

Flyer and I will be hanging for a couple of days until he and his dad go to Maine to visit family. I'll be glad to get a break from the losers at school. "Hey . . . J-J-Jed. What's . . . up . . . dude?" Luckily every time Jackson and his buddies open their stupid mouths, Flyer tells them to shut up. They know about my brother Zeke. Can't they cut me some slack?

As for the documentary, I'm not sure I know which story it is I would tell, as Ms. Conrad says, or even if I have a story at all, but for Velly's sake, I'll look.

★ ★ ★

On the sidewalk, people dart around us. Yellow taxis speed. Buses screech and groan. A CACOPH-ONY OF COLOR AND SOUND.

Those words, along with pages of others, are safe inside my messenger bag. My brother Zeke was a poet. He called himself Bird, after the late great alto sax player Charlie "Bird" Parker. He said he liked to improvise with words the way Charlie did with notes.

Flyer's eyes go judgmental whenever he dips in and sees Zeke's notebook. Like I am the sorriest brother ever. Like I'm Linus dragging some rag of a blanket till I'm thirteen.

As if Flyer doesn't clutch that key chain of his mother's like it's his last ice pick on an Everest as-cent. He's just lucky that I'm a big enough dude not to mention it.

Flyer leans down. He peers at the 3 × 4 camera

screen, where a bike messenger has a near miss with a stroller. The kid's baby-sitter shouts at the biker, her thick West Indian accent melting into the swirl of a siren somewhere in the distance.

"Live-action video, ladies and gentlemen, by film master Jed." Flyer messes my hair. Then he takes the camera. He trains the lens on me. "This is Joseph Eli Diamond," he says.

I scowl at him for using my real name on camera.

"Aka J. E. D. Juvenile Educational Dreamboat. But call him Jed. Jed the dread head. Jed the old-movie fanatic, the stud forward for Man Prep b-ball, the phatty-phat photographer, the best bud to the soon-to-be-famous Flyer Gray."

He skates slow circles around me. My black boots chuff the pavement. I manage a small smile.

Flyer shouldn't lie on film. I suck at basketball. Once I subbed half a period as forward because Pasqual Ravo started puking his brains out and, by some miracle, I finessed a killer layup. Most of the time my butt was on the bench. My hair is kind of long and dark like Mom's before she went gray, but the dreadlocks are a pipe dream. Dad would make me go all military if I even so much as tried. I love taking pictures, but my photos aren't that good. Plus, everyone knows my grades are in the toilet this year, and they were never that great to begin with. The strong sibling policy at Manhattan Prep accounts for my spot.

My turn.

Flyer waits for me to focus. Then he waits for me to speak.

"Theo." That's all that comes. I feel my face redden. Words fight for space in my mouth. Which is so stupid. I can always talk to Flyer.

"I'm Theodore Alexander Gray the Second," Flyer finishes. "Native New Yorker, Sagittarius, skateboard prodigy, candy connoisseur, filmmaker-to-watch."

15

A short laugh trips up my throat. Only a dude as cool as Flyer would rib himself for you. He hates his name, too.

Flyer smacks his grape gum. Kicks up the front of his board. Pivots and powerslides before spinning a full 360. He wags his board up and down to say yes. He flashes a peace sign and rakes ring-studded fingers through his bleached hair, where black roots poke up.

Then we sail up the sidewalk, searching for subjects.

# "SCRAPPLE FROM THE APPLE"

"'Art imitates life,'" Flyer chants up Avenue A. Past delis and cafés. Video stores and juice bars. Tattoo parlors and vintage clothing shops.

"Or was it 'life imitates art'?" he muses. "Now I can't remember what Velly said. Who cares? We're going to create a real work of art that imitates nothing and no one."

"True that," I say.

In reality, Flyer's not that good with the camera. He never showed a real interest in film till his mom left. It doesn't matter. I plan to do most of the camera work. I'm hoping it will give Dad and me something to connect on. He always takes vacation around the holidays. Since we're not going skiing this year, maybe we'll get some hang time

17

here in New York — going to movies and the planetarium, losing ourselves in bookstores and then chowing down on sushi — like we used to do once upon a time.

Flyer and I weave up our favorite streets. I whistle whenever he's about to skate into a pile of dog crap. Call it a sixth sense, but I always know when crap is near, even when I'm not looking down at the pavement.

The air is thick with candied nuts and sirens. All the stores look like they're dressed up for one of Dad's black-tie charity events.

We stop at Kim's Video, where I rent all my movies. Red, green, and gold lights wink on and off. A tall woman in tight jeans and cowboy boots emerges. Shop bells jingle in her wake. She flashes a grin at the camera, then blows an air kiss my way. My heart pounds as she disappears up the street.

"Yo, she digs you, man." Flyer smirks.

Yeah, right. The last girlfriend I had was

Penelope Li, in sixth grade. A beautiful girl. But she was all prudish and broke up with me when I tried to tongue kiss her. These days, I'd pretty much given up on girls anyway. I could just see myself trying to cough up the words to ask someone out as a whole hallway of kids roared with laughter. If I weren't Jewish, I might consider monkhood.

We walk past the fire station, the Hells Angels headquarters, mosaic-tiled streetlamps, decaying brownstones, and new high-rises. We know where we're heading without even saying it.

Around us, BIKE MESSENGERS BOB THROUGH TRAFFIC, FIRE ESCAPES SNAKE DOWN BUILDINGS, and OLD WOMEN LEAN ON WEARY PILLOWS / IN FIRST-FLOOR WINDOWS / WATCHING THE HYPNOTIC TICKTOCK OF VILLAGE LIFE. Lots of images in Zeke's notebook are easy to spot. Others are nowhere, like STREET ANGELS and some mystery girl whose eyes HAUNT MY DREAMS.

19

Sometimes I think I see Zeke, his shiny black hair like a crow's wing, or his bouncy walk. Sometimes I hear his deep laugh rising up from a group of kids. The worst is when my mind starts in with its tricks, making me wonder if it really is him.

Above us, cylindrical wooden water towers perch on rooftops. They are beautiful beings, sturdy and proud. They stand on black steel legs. Pointy caps dot their heads. On some buildings, there are clusters of towers — a tall mom and squat father, huddled around two babies. On others, there's just A SOLITARY TOWER, PRESSED FIRMLY INTO THE SKYLINE, A THUMBPRINT OF OUR CITY.

Sometimes I imagine that the towers are rockets, ready to launch into space. Sometimes I wish I could lift off with them.

I find the lone tower on top of my building and I follow the sound of Flyer's skateboard wheels as I tilt the lens skyward to film it.

Once, Flyer and I snuck up to the roof and caught Zeke climbing the ladder up the tower. As soon as he saw us, he came back down. He looked like we'd just walked in on him in the bathroom or something. "Don't you ever go up there!" he'd shouted in my face. "I'll have to hurt you if you do. I mean it. It's dangerous."

"What were you doing?" I'd asked.

He grabbed a fistful of my jacket, just below my neck. "I better not find you on the roof again. I'm older. I'm allowed up here."

I wasn't stupid. I knew that wasn't true. For one thing, Zeke was only four years older. And, anyway, *no one* was allowed on the roof. There was a building rule against it. "Liability," Dad said. "We're responsible if someone gets hurt or falls off."

As I'm filming the tower, a bird circles the tip. Its wings are so vast that I move the camera to check it out, but the bird is already gone.

We arrive at Jesus by the park. Jesus, with his sad eyes and his dripping wounds, is encased in a big glass box in someone's front courtyard. There's a tiny latch on the door. Plastic flowers, stuffed animals, torn-out psalms, burning candles all surround Jesus' limp feet. Letters and prayers and crayon pictures from little kids are taped inside and out. It makes my heart sting so much, I turn off the camera. And like I said, I'm Jewish.

Or at least we were Jewish until July, when Zeke died and Dad renounced religion. Not just for himself, but for the whole family. My bar mitzvah was supposed to have been this past fall — October 12, to be exact.

That morning at breakfast, Mom had said, "I'm sorry, Joseph."

For some reason, I started thinking about Zeke's bar mitzvah, how he based his sermon on the writings of the prophet Ezekiel and ended with a poem he'd written:

MAY I BECOME
A MAN
AS GREAT AS MY FATHER
AND HIS FATHER
BEFORE HIM
OR GREATER STILL.

There was more to it, but those are the lines I remember. Zeke winked at Dad on the last line, and
Rabbi David and the rest of the sanctuary bubbled
up with warm laughter. It made me proud and
also excited for the day when I'd be up on the
bimah, reading from the Torah in front of all my
friends and family for the first time. It made me so
anxious to cross that invisible line, as Zeke had.

Mom reached across the breakfast table to
squeeze my forearm. I wanted to ask her why she
never took a stronger stand with Dad, why Rabbi
David was the only one who'd really tried. But instead I pulled my arm away. Mom got a hurt look

23

on her face, so I tried to make it seem like I was just taking a bite of cereal, but I knew she saw through me.

"If people name their kids Jesus and Allah," I suddenly hear Flyer saying, "why don't they name them God?"

As I chew on Flyer's question, I finger the carved-metal bird hanging from a leather cord around my neck. I never take it off. Velly gave it to me in September.

"It's a *milagro*," Velly had said. "A charm, a petition to the saints to keep you safe. My father was a metalsmith in Ecuador. He taught me to make these. I carved a bird for you because it can take you to higher places, help you soar. You may feel grounded now and for a while. Grief has its own mind and its own timetable. But, *por favor, amigo,* don't forget your wings.

"Look at our city, put to the test in the most painful and profound way, but beginning to rise again. You, too, will rise again. You must. It's the only way to honor what you've lost.

"Keep this *milagro* close and it will protect you, *amigo*. *Te lo prometo*. I promise."

I got a lump in my throat. "I'm not . . . the one . . . who needed protecting."

Velly put a hand on my shoulder. "We all need protecting, *amigo*."

We both shut up after that. Which was just as well, because Mom doesn't want me talking about Zeke. She says family business should stay in the family.

I fish in the pocket of my jeans and pull out a Super Ball with swirls of blue, green, and brown colors. It looks like the world. I kiss it, then open the door to the glass box and place it at the bottom, near Jesus' feet, in between a candle and a stack of baseball cards. Call me corny.

Some of Zeke's other stuff is still here — a Matchbox car, a ceramic paperweight, his diabetes

25

I.D. bracelet, which he never wore, anyway — but most of it is gone: books, his toothbrush, his wool hat. I figure either Jesus spirited them off to Zeke somewhere or they're with someone who needs them. Better that than me having to look at them and get that raw, burning feeling in my chest.

Flyer digs in one of the side pockets of his cargo pants and comes up with the tiniest flashlight you've ever seen. He turns it on and puts it next to the Super Ball. It lights up a patch that looks like Australia, as well as a bird feather.

Just as the raw feeling starts to worm its way through my insides, Flyer says, "Come on, soldier. I'm starving."

# "LA PALOMA"

The camera is back on, eating up images, as we make our way over to the café where we hang. I am just about to turn it off when a waify homeless girl pops onto the screen. She is slumped in the doorway next to our café. A caramel-colored dog, about the size of my messenger bag, is circled on a blanket beside her, its head resting on one of her boots. A small cardboard sign on the ground in front of them reads: TRAVELING. NEED HELP.

"What up?" I whisper to Flyer.

"She's a space cowgirl, dude." He keeps his voice low too, so the girl can't hear.

I've got a minute of footage before I realize the camera is still running. I quickly shut it off, but my feet are glued to the sidewalk. The girl looks

27

up and locks into my gaze. She's got these huge gray eyes that take up most of her face. Her ash-colored hair sticks up in spiky clumps. She's pretty in a strange kind of way.

Flyer moves past her and heads for the door. He holds it open. "Coming, Jed?" he asks.

The girl shakes the coins in her cup. I pull a dollar from the front pocket of my jeans and stuff it in.

Inside, the beautiful Melody floats from one end of the counter to the other. Her long amber curls bounce like Slinkies around her shining face, and the tiny diamond stud on the side of her nose glistens. When she sees us she smiles and waves one long, wand-like arm to motion us over.

"Well, if it isn't the Frog Footman and the Fish Footman." A bubble of laughter pops from her mouth.

I once told her that *Alice in Wonderland* was my favorite book when I was a kid. Turns out it was her favorite, too.

But Melody's not laughing to make fun of me. She's laughing because she always laughs. Even when nothing's funny.

"Dude, she's sixteen," Flyer has said more than once. "There's, like, no chance she'd ever be interested in an eighth grader."

Who says I'm even interested. If you ask me, Flyer can get a little bent out of shape for nothing. Even if I did like Melody, I wasn't stupid enough to think that she'd go out with me. Especially now that I really was croaking like the Frog Footman.

Flyer and I unload our stuff on a chair in the corner and climb onto two stools while Melody clears a scatter of dirty dishes. All around us are mismatched tables, lamps, chairs, and sofas from the flea market up the street. Paintings from local artists hang on the walls, along with announcements for concerts, apartments, art exhibits, writing workshops, and trips abroad. Styles and colors collide in a way that would drive my mom crazy. But I like it.

In a few minutes we're eating our sandwiches in silence. Food is sacred for Flyer and me. We almost never interrupt a good meal with mindless chatter.

While I eat, I watch Melody drift back and forth from the tables to the counter. Björk's haunting voice on the stereo melts into every corner of the room as the Elvis clock above the espresso machine rocks out time.

For some reason, Jamal's words drift back into my head: *"New York City ain't no place to be careless."*

I think about the drunk guy on the subway platform. *"Yer suppos'ta ask someone's permission be-*

*fore you film them.*" It's true that I didn't ask his permission. Which is funny, because I did ask for Jamal's. I didn't ask the homeless girl, either, but I wouldn't think about filming Melody without making sure she was okay with it. Why is that? Was I being careless?

Melody comes over to clear our dishes and motions with her chin to the camera on the counter next to us. "You guys pretending to be tourists?" She laughs.

"We're on assignment," Flyer says, as if he actually does work as a documentary filmmaker along with his mom.

One of Melody's amber-colored eyebrows arches slightly. "Really."

I want to talk to her, to tell her all about Velly's assignment, but I'm certain as soon as I open my mouth, my words are going to trip all over one another. "Sort of," I manage.

Melody is smiling this huge smile, like she's genuinely excited to hear whatever it is I have to say. If only I could say it.

"For school. We-we-we-" I'm not stuttering, I just can't move off the word.

"We're making a documentary of the neighborhood for school," Flyer tells her.

"Cool," she says. Her pale green eyes glow. "So I assume you're lining up people to interview?"

Flyer and I look at her blankly.

"What do you mean?" Flyer asks. "We're just going to get footage of the neighborhood."

"Oh," she says, sounding sort of disappointed. "I guess that'll work." She wipes the counter in front of us with a damp rag.

"What?" I ask.

"I just think it would be more interesting if you talked to people. You know, Frog," she urges, "like Alice. Talk to the Mock Turtle. Talk to the

Duchess and the Cheshire Cat. Ask them about their life histories."

When Melody disappears to the other end of the counter, Flyer turns to me. "What on earth is she talking about?"

I think of Alice, traveling with the Gryphon.

*They had not gone very far before they saw the Mock Turtle in the distance, sitting sad and lonely on a little ledge of rock, and, as they came nearer, Alice could hear him sighing as if his heart would break. She pitied him deeply. "What is his sorrow?" she asked the Gryphon. . . .*

I don't even realize I've muttered the last line aloud until Melody turns from where she is making a cappuccino. "'It's all his fancy, that . . .'"

"'He hasn't got no sorrow,'" we say together.

"I never understood that line," Melody says.

"Everyone's got sorrow. It's probably the only real thing we all have in common." She says this last part with an odd laugh.

"You're both crazy," Flyer says.

"No." Melody grins. "We're both . . ." She pauses for me to chime in with her.

"MAD!" we say together.

Flyer rolls his eyes and slurps down the last of his grape soda. "Somebody please help me."

# "THINGS TO COME"

## FIVE

"What's wrong, Jedi?" Flyer asks when we step out into the cold afternoon air.

The doorway next to the café is empty. The homeless girl and her dog are gone.

"You wanted to interview her?" Flyer asks.

I nod.

"She's just some druggie." Flyer busts a manual. He balances on the tail of his skateboard and points the nose skyward like a rocket.

I turn on the camera and film the empty spot.

HER HARD-SOFT EYES HAUNT MY DREAMS. . . .

Could the girl Flyer and I saw earlier be the one Zeke wrote about?

My shot is nothing but pavement, two concrete steps, and a steel door. There are a bunch of

35

nickels scattered on the sidewalk, and then I notice something on the bottom step. I zoom in closer. It's a comb, black and narrow, with some scratches on the sides and a few teeth missing in the middle.

Faintly I hear Flyer's skate wheels scrape the pavement. Then two feet pop onto my screen. A hand reaches down. It grabs the comb.

When I look up, the homeless girl is staring me in the face.

"You shouldn't film people without asking. It's rude." Her voice is rough, like a bus grinding its breaks.

She stuffs the comb into her back pocket, turns with the dog, and disappears around the corner. She doesn't even pick up the nickels.

For a moment, I just stare at the empty doorway again. And suddenly, it hits me.

The comb.

It looks like Zeke's.

* * *

"You really think it was the one you put there?"
Flyer is asking. We're sitting on a bench inside the
dog run at Tompkins Square Park.

CHARLiE'S PARK
CHARLiE PARKER'S PARK
PARK YOURSELF AND LiSTEN TO CHARLiE
THE JAZZ MAN
THE BEBOP KiNG
THE BEST SAXOPHONiST TO EVER LiVE
OR DiE.

In my head, I can see Zeke sliding his fingers
across an invisible sax, then getting up and bopping around his room. I'd grab a ruler off his desk,
pop it between my lips, and puff out my cheeks
like Dizzy Gillespie, his trumpeter and tight pal.
And for a little while, we'd be two mad-good horn
players chasing notes and reinventing sound.

37

A pigeon forages for food by my feet and wakes me out of my memory. Old men play checkers on the concrete tables by the fence. Above us, a chalk smudge of moon hangs in the sky.

"I don't want to sound like a jerk," Flyer says, "but aren't there a thousand black combs like that one?"

It is crazy, I guess, thinking that this homeless girl has Zeke's comb. I can't even remember when I stopped seeing it by Jesus' feet, or if I stopped seeing it. But it's gone now. We checked before coming here. Why do I even care?

Flyer pulls a purple bandanna from his pocket and cleans the front truck of his skateboard. "If you really think it's Zeke's comb, we can track her down and get it back," he says.

"Nah."

"Yeah, what are the chances it's his anyway?"

I'm pretty sure the comb is Zeke's. But so what?

The clang of the gate interrupts my thoughts.

A large woman with slightly bulging eyes and bow lips enters. She's walking so many dogs, she looks like Santa Claus steering a team of reindeer.

"Hold your horses, now, and let me shut the gate," she says. The remnants of a British accent leak through on every other word. "Quiet, Sophie. You know it isn't ladylike to whine like you are. Now let me untie you before you knot yourselves up splendidly."

THE QUEEN OF CANINES REIGNS OVER HER RETAINERS. . . .

Magically, the dogs all form a circle around her and wait as she unclips their leashes. Their tails sweep little dust clouds into the air.

The woman crosses the dog run, sits on a bench beside ours, and snaps open a newspaper.

I turn on the camera and film the dogs.

"They all have agents, you know. Sophie's is out in Hollywood, Olivia's, too, come to think of it. Burt, the shepherd, now his rep is here in New

York." The woman peers out from behind her newspaper and smirks. "All currently out of work, as well. But they're available for commercials, sit-coms, movies, you name it."

Flyer laughs. "How 'bout interviews?"

"Of course. They love interviews." The woman lays down her newspaper. "Who would you like?"

Flyer and I check out the cluster of dogs. I point to a red-and-white one with long ears.

"Excellent choice. She's mine. Ella!" the woman calls.

The dog trots over. She hops up onto the bench and sits next to the woman. I center them on my screen.

"These two boys would like to ask you some questions, Sweetums, so be polite, and no drool-ing, please." The dog licks the woman's ear. A small giggle escapes from her mouth. She turns Ella to face the camera.

Ella lifts her right paw. Flyer holds out a hand

to shake it. "So Ella," he says. "What do you like most about living in the East Village?"

Ella sniffs the air.

The woman smiles. "She says it's the splendid array of smells."

"You've got to be joking," Flyer says.

Ella sniffs again.

"The sidewalks alone are a tapestry of food scraps, canine elimination, chewing gum, cigarette butts, inky papers, decayed leaves, old shoes, lost toys. Such diversity."

"All right, what do you like least?"

Ella barks.

"That would be the noise, sirens especially. They hurt my ears. I also loathe car alarms and the drunken shrieks of young people. The occasional gunshot is particularly nerve-splintering."

"Yeah, I know what you mean," Flyer says. "How 'bout your favorite food?"

Ella's tongue lolls out the side of her mouth as

41

she watches the other dogs chase a ratty tennis ball.

"Even though I could travel to every culinary continent in a few square blocks, when it comes right down to it, I'm a simple gal. My favorite food is pizza."

"True that, true that. How long have you lived here?"

"We came across the pond from London in sixty-eight. I was going to be a singer and a performance artist. I married my best friend, Eddie, to get a green card. He was the gentlest soul I'd ever met. I was in love with him. But Eddie did not care for girls other than in a friend sort of way, if you know what I mean. I nursed him through a long, terrible illness, then became a widow at twenty-four. The rest, well, the rest isn't worth mentioning, really. That was the defining part of my life."

"Wow, you've had it rough. I can relate." Ella

licks Flyer's hand, then hops off the bench and runs over to a fat Labrador rolling in the dirt.

I lay the camera on my leg.

The woman leans over to look at me. "Don't you have anything to say?"

I shrug.

"Jed's a little shy," Flyer tells her.

"Yes, well, I can see there's a lot going on inside you, Jed."

I feel my neck get hot.

"You've got quite a face, love. Like a message written in code. You look a bit like my Eddie. If you don't mind my saying so, you might want to let someone crack you one day. I've always wondered if that would have made a difference for my Eddie."

5:00 P.M.

# "BIRD'S NEST"

The apartment is empty when I get home. The first thing I do is trip over one of Leo's ambulances.

Ambulances are the only toys Leo will play with. He's always making loud siren noises and rushing them through the apartment, trying to get them to the hospital before the patient dies.

I hang my jacket on a hook in the foyer, kick my shoes into the bin Mom has placed here so we don't track dirt into the apartment. Flyer let me keep the camera overnight. I turn it on and head down the short hallway, through the big living room where two white sofas face off in silence and Mom's baby grand sits mute.

I grab an apple from a bowl on the kitchen

counter and eat with my left hand while I film with my right. There used to be a wall separating the kitchen from a formal dining room, but Mom had the top half of the wall torn out and turned the dining room into a den. Redecorating used to occupy a lot of her time.

We live on the third floor of an old six-story building. The rooms are big, and the walls have chunky decorative moldings. Supposedly a conductor for the New York Philharmonic grew up here, which Mom loves because she teaches music history at Hunter College and is a classically trained pianist. Her beautiful Beethoven sonatas used to curl out the window to greet me when I got home from school.

I've tried to introduce Mom to newer styles of music. But she always says the same thing: "I like music that's organized and anticipatory. I like when it has clean lines and resolves at the end."

That pretty much sums up Mom. Beyond the occasional ambulance, there is no clutter anywhere in our apartment. Books are shelved alphabetically by author and subject or are stacked in purposeful piles on coffee tables; newspapers have their own special crates (though they never accumulate long enough to fill them); and there are closets for coats, bins for shoes, a cabinet for CDs and videos, separate baskets for incoming and outgoing mail, hooks for keys, and files for just about everything, from book reviews to museum hours to recipes. Sometimes I feel like I'm living inside a Palm Pilot.

Even though we almost never get drop-in visitors, Mom wants the apartment looking "presentable" (read: ready for a spontaneous *Architectural Digest* shoot) at all times. I can keep my room how I want it, as long as the door is shut.

Off the kitchen is another hallway, where all the bedrooms are: first mine and Leo's on one side, separated by a bathroom, then Mom and Dad's on the other side, and Zeke's at the end of the hall. All the rooms sort of shoot off to the left and right of the living room. Dad says that the floor plan of our apartment looks like a uterus and fallopian tubes, which is a totally weird way to think about it, if you ask me, but that's the kind of stuff you get when your dad delivers babies for a living.

One of the doctors in the obstetrics department at Dad's hospital, St. Vincent's, hosted a dinner for him a few months ago, in honor of his 500th delivery. We all went. At one point, a bunch of people clinked their glasses for Dad to say something. He was gripping his glass a little too tightly, and some wine sloshed over the sides when he stood up. I could see a tiny muscle in the side of his neck pulsing like a rapid heartbeat. There were a few awkward moments of quiet before he finally spoke.

"There is no greater honor than bringing life into this world. That's why I became a doctor, because of how much I value life." Dad smiled uneasily, then sat back down.

Everyone at the dinner knew about Zeke's death, of course, so there was another uncomfortable silence after that.

Then Mom started clapping really loudly until everyone else joined in.

I've always wondered what Dad meant. That he was still a good doctor? That Zeke's death shouldn't be a reflection on him? That Zeke didn't value life?

I keep the camera running as I wander down the hall to his room. Not that we've ever discussed it, but there's sort of an unspoken understanding that Zeke's room is sacred and, therefore, off-limits.

The door is shut as usual, and I gently push it open. The room is bigger than mine and has two long windows, so the light is better, too. I'd always thought I'd move in here after Zeke left for college.

Against the far wall, in between the windows, is the trundle bed, with its blue bedspread pulled neat and taut. I remember Zeke showing me how to build forts by hanging blankets and sleeping bags from the backs of chairs and then squaring them off between the bed and desk. It was in one of those forts, by flashlight, that he taught me how to tie my shoes and play gin rummy and read.

When Zeke and I were little, I'd sometimes sleep in the bottom bed. If I had a nightmare, I always came in here instead of going to my parents' room. Which is funny, because in the past couple of years before he died, Zeke sometimes scared me. His stormy moods could kick up out of nowhere. Especially at dinner when Dad made him report his glucose levels.

One of the worst fights was on my twelfth

birthday. Zeke seemed to have a way of picking important occasions to lose it.

That afternoon, he had promised to take me to see the Everest movie at the IMAX theater uptown. I think Mom assumed we'd be traveling together, but he told me to meet him there at 3:00. I rode the train about sixty blocks and waited out front. Three o'clock came, then 3:15, when the movie started, but still no sign of Zeke. At 3:30, I started to worry that maybe he'd gone into insulin shock or something on his way up here. By 4:00, I was on the verge of calling Mom, except I knew she'd freak about me being alone and about what could have happened to Zeke. Finally, around 4:10, Zeke showed up with some girl.

"Hey, little brother, happy birthday," he said. "Sorry we're late. This is Jasmine."

"Happy birthday." She smiled. She had wide dark eyes, two long black braids, and a killer grin. She was probably the hottest girl I'd ever seen.

"Where were you? I got scared something happened," I said to Zeke.

He slung one arm over my shoulder and the other over Jasmine's. "Don't worry so much. We can still make the next show." Zeke shepherded us inside and bought us popcorn and Milk Duds and sodas. When the movie ended, he said good-bye to Jasmine and took me to this huge arcade in Midtown. After that, we walked all the way home, and on the way Zeke let me puff my first cigar. He told me that as soon as I was old enough, he was going to take me traveling, in Europe or South America. "Just you and me in the big, wide world, little dude."

I could hardly wait for that day.

We were late getting back for my birthday dinner, but I didn't care. I was having such a good time that I'd forgotten all about being mad at Zeke for showing up late.

Mom had made my favorite meal, chicken

curry, and everything was going fine until Dad started in with the blood sugar interrogation.

"What's my sugar?" Zeke said. "Oh, I much prefer Domino over the generic brands. It has a much finer crystal. How 'bout you, Leo? Strained peas with sugar or without?" Zeke leaned over and tenderly wiped a smear of green mush off Leo's cheek.

Leo babbled and laughed.

"And you, Joseph?" Zeke asked.

I couldn't help but crack a smile.

"Have you guys seen Joseph's latest photos from school?" Zeke continued casually. "They're amazing!"

I felt my whole body puff up with pride.

But Dad leveled a look at Zeke and told him to stop dodging the question. His voice was always harsh, unrelenting. "You've got to take responsibility!"

"Honey, this is for your own good," Mom said more gently.

"No, it's not. It's for your peace of mind."

"Ezekiel, don't talk that way to your mother."

"Robert, why can't you just trust me?" Zeke said.

"We do." Mom reached out a hand to him, then gave Dad a look that said he should say so too.

"Fine," Dad answered. You could feel him backing away, acting like he didn't care, which was worse than him being angry. "It's your life."

Anger rose inside Zeke like a volcano. "Yeah, it is, so why don't you let me live it?!" He slammed his fork on the table and then got up and put his fist through the wall.

You could have choked on the silence that followed.

Before Zeke fled the apartment, he tossed back a number — 100, 125, something in the normal range — but it was hard to know if he was telling the truth or not.

53

At this point, Leo started wailing, and Mom picked him up and took him into the den to settle him.

"Why can't you ever cut him any slack?" I asked Dad. "It's not his fault he has diabetes. He's smart. He knows what he needs to do to take care of himself. You treat him like a baby."

I don't know if it was the sharp tone of my voice or the surprise of hearing me talk back or the fact that it was my birthday, but Dad just took the hit of those words. I even saw his chest cave a little, as if I had landed a fist there. He got up and walked slowly to the kitchen door. "You might see things differently when you're a parent," he said finally, his voice punctured.

Later, while Mom and I ate my cake alone in the kitchen, she said, "Will you talk to your brother? He respects you, Joseph. You can get through to him in ways Dad and I can't."

"I'll try," I said, feeling the burden of that responsibility like a 500-pound weight on my chest.

But it turned out Mom was wrong about Zeke listening to me. Maybe he was sick of everyone focusing on what was wrong instead of what was right. Maybe he just didn't want to hear it from his little brother. Maybe if I'd said it better, he'd still be here.

I fall onto the bed and look around at the posters of Charlie Parker, Kurt Cobain, and Janis Joplin; poetry books by Lord Byron and John Keats; the basketball trophies; the signed basketball from Michael Jordan that Zeke bought on eBay; his collection of snow globes on a shelf by the bed; the incense burner; the patchouli incense cones; the self-timed photo I shot of all of us in Stowe; and the nearly empty ladder of CDs.

I took most of the CDs and Zeke's poetry

notebook, which I don't think Mom and Dad even knew about. After the funeral, I snuck in here and slept on the bottom bed. I read *Alice in Wonderland* late into the night because even though I was exhausted from talking to the million people who had come by with food and apologies that afternoon, it was hard to fall asleep. Somehow it was comforting to read about Alice in all those crazy situations, to see her maneuver through them, and know she'd wake up and everything would be okay again.

I didn't find the notebook, buried under the mattress, until the next morning when I made the bed. I'd forgotten all about it.

The notebook was small — the size of a paperback novel — and was spiral bound, with a purplish blue cardboard cover. Zeke had shared pieces of it with me, but never the whole book. I took it into my room to read.

There was one poem I really liked:

## ODE ON A WOODEN WATER TOWER

WITH APOLOGIES TO MR. JOHN KEATS

O UNDISCOVERED BRIDE OF SOLITUDE!
O LOST COUSIN OF NATURE AND WATERS DEEP
WOODLAND HISTORIAN WHO CANNOT EXUDE
THE STORY OF YOUR JOURNEY HERE, LEST
    WE WEEP
WHAT MEMORIES — FORESTS, OCEANS —
    HAUNT YOUR SHAPE. . . .
WHAT SCARS DO YOU BEAR? WHAT GHOSTS
    LINGER IN YOUR WALLS?
WHEN WE ARE DUST AND ASH UPON THE
    EARTH YOU SHALL REMAIN — A BEACON,
    A GLIMMER IN THE MIDST OF WOE
A FRIEND TO THOSE WHO SEEK YOU. . . .

And another that really got to me:

MY BODY
   FIERCE
   LEAN
   MUSCLED
   TOWERING
   BROKEN

I've never told Mom and Dad about the note-book. I just want something of his that's all mine.

I feel my throat start to close. I make myself cough so I don't cry. I pick up the snow globe from Stowe, Vermont, where we used to go skiing every December.

Back in June, when Mom was calling the lodge to reserve our rooms for this year, Zeke said since he was a senior he'd want to be in New York with his friends for New Year's Eve. Because it was Zeke asking, Mom and Dad said okay and moved our trip to February. They were always bending over backwards to give him his way, as if they were trying to make up for the fact that he was defective or something. He was never expected to baby-sit for Leo the way I was. The rules were always different for Zeke.

I can't help but look at the bed where I'm sitting. Suddenly the horror of finding him comes flooding back. I turn off the camera.

On the Fourth of July, a few weeks after Zeke had that convo with Mom, we all went to see fireworks — me with Flyer and his dad down in Battery Park; Mom, Dad, and Leo with Aunt Jane and my cousin, Violet, in East River Park; and Zeke with a bunch of friends on somebody's rooftop. He was already asleep when Mom, Dad, and Leo got home around midnight. The next morning, everyone, including Dad, slept in. He had taken the day off work and was just getting up when I got home from sleeping at Flyer's. Dad went in to wake Zeke for the brunch we'd planned at home, and I followed because I wanted to hear about Zeke's night. It only took Dad a second to realize something was wrong. All the color was drained from Zeke's face. It had an empty, surprised expression. Dad immediately threw off the covers and started feeling for a pulse.

"Joseph, go get me a glass of orange juice! Get your mother and call 911. Now!"

I ran to the kitchen, told Mom, and made the phone call. Then I grabbed Leo.

"Oh, my God!" Mom was screaming when I got back to Zeke's room.

"Lilah, please! He's going to be fine!"

Dad pried open Zeke's mouth and poured in the orange juice. But it just dribbled out the sides and spilled down his cheeks.

Dad was still giving Zeke mouth-to-mouth when the paramedics got there. There was a blond guy with a beard and a black guy with a shaved head. The black guy leaned down and took over the chest compressions while Dad continued with the breathing. The blond guy asked Dad a bunch of questions in between breaths, then radioed the hospital and relayed the situation. He started an I.V. line and set up the gurney.

When the paramedics lifted Zeke onto the gurney and hooked up the oxygen, Dad grabbed the sides of his head and spun in slow circles before folding in on himself like a totaled car. Mom started gasping for breath.

All this time, I hovered in the doorway, holding Leo. I felt hollow, as if only a shell of me were standing there while the rest of me floated over the scene, trying to take it all in.

As the paramedics wheeled Zeke out the door, I saw them exchange a look, and the blond guy shook his head slightly. They told Mom and Dad to follow them in a taxi to St. Vincent's emergency room.

Leo started wailing. I took him into his room. I didn't know what else to do, so I started reading him *The Carrot Seed*.

A few minutes later, Mom came in and hugged both of us. She seemed calmer. She asked if I'd be all right until they got back. Leo kept reaching up for her, but she didn't seem to see him.

"He's gone?" I asked.

Mom pursed her lips and fought back tears. "We don't know that. He could be fine. He's getting the best possible care, the best."

"What happened?"

She shook her head. "Janey will be here soon. I'll call you from the hospital."

Zeke had gone into insulin shock before, from not eating enough or from waiting too long to eat after he'd taken his insulin. Once when I was in fifth grade, Zeke baby-sat for me while Mom and Dad went to some black-tie dinner. They'd left us money to order pizza. But when it came, Zeke just guzzled one of Dad's beers and didn't touch the pie.

Dad had taught me how to give Zeke an injection in case of an emergency. He described the warning signs for various scenarios and what first steps to take to help Zeke. "Hypoglycemia, or insulin shock, is the most immediate danger," he had explained. "Because the window of time to help is very small. Always call 911 if he doesn't improve immediately."

"You need to take your insulin, and you need to eat," I'd told Zeke as I watched him pop open another beer.

"I'm fine, little bro. Don't worry so much."

We were watching *NYPD Blue* on a small TV we'd brought into the kitchen. My eyes kept traveling back and forth from the set to Zeke. When he started to sweat and breathe faster, I jumped up and got him a glass of orange juice and a

63

Hershey's bar from the pantry where Mom kept a stash.

By this time, his hands were shaking so much, I had to help him drink the juice. I could tell he was in bad shape, because he didn't fight me.

A few minutes later, he shook his head and smiled. "Guess I just got a little tipsy. I didn't think I was such a lightweight."

Later Zeke took me out to shoot pool, even though Mom and Dad had told us to stay in. While we were playing, Zeke said, "Don't tell them about my little dizzy spell, okay? They'll just worry over nothing."

I remember feeling like the coolest dude on earth out at a pool hall on a Saturday night when I was only ten. Mom and Dad would never have allowed that. If it weren't for Zeke, I probably would have turned out to be pretty lame. "I won't tell," I'd told him.

My throat contracts again. The thrashing voice inside me starts shouting: *Why weren't you here why weren't you here why weren't you here?!*

I shake my head and then the snow globe. I watch as the white flakes shimmy over Stowe Peak and settle softly around the lodge at the base of the mountain.

A tear lands on my hand. I put the snow globe back on the shelf and straighten the bedspread. Then I pick up the camera and quietly cross the room to the door.

As I'm leaving, I notice something colorful stuck behind the wastebasket under the desk. I bend down to get a closer look.

It's one of Leo's ambulances.

## SEVEN

6:00 P.M.

# "LEO THE LION"

I'm on my bed, listening to Charlie Parker. His swirling sax used to pour out of Zeke's room down the hall to mine. When I pop in a Bird CD, it's like I can feel myself filling up with Zeke.

Today, Bird's music also makes me think of his house on Charlie Parker Place, on the east side of the park. That makes me think of the Queen and her dogs. I am just remembering the weird thing she said about my face when I hear Mom and Leo come through the door.

As always, Leo's feet pad down the hallway like a soft drumbeat. I step out of my room to greet him.

"Yoseph!" He beams.

"Leo!" I answer. I pick him up and swing him

around. He has trouble with his *j*'s. He's only two and a half. He doesn't know that Yosef is my Hebrew name.

Leo throws his arms around my neck.

I kiss his cold red cheek.

He squirms a little, so I put him down. He grabs my hand. "Yoseph, come play."

I step back into my room to turn off the stereo, with Leo still clinging to my hand. Then I follow him into the kitchen, where Mom is unpacking groceries. "Hi, Mom," I say.

"Hi, Mom," Leo echoes as he trots into the den.

I try to keep my sentences short. When Mom noticed I was having trouble talking in September, she went into overdrive and tried to send me to the speech therapist at school.

"I'm fine," I told her.

Thankfully she hasn't had the energy to fight me on it.

It also helps that she thinks I've been going through a quiet, sullen phase ever since I turned thirteen in October, which, she says, launched me "full throttle into adolescence."

Why are adults so obsessed with adolescence? It's not as if teenagers walk around analyzing the phases of their midlife crises — like Mom's friend Allie Klein getting Botox lips, or Dad suddenly becoming obsessed with developing a monster body.

Like we're the only ones trying to figure out who we are. Yeah, right.

Velly would scan our list of vocabulary words and say that's a good example of *irony*.

"How was school, honey?" Mom asks.

"I'm on . . . vacation?"

Mom forces a light laugh. "Where is my head?" Normally she and Leo would be on winter break now, too — she from teaching, and he from day care. But they've been on a four-month leave since Mom took this semester off.

I start unloading food into the pantry next to the table while she folds the paper bags and tucks them neatly under the sink.

"Where did you and Theo go today?"

"Around." Mom likes to pretend that I have more freedom than I actually do. We both know that she's imposed boundaries, from Fourteenth Street to Houston going north-south, and from Avenue A to Third going east-west. Flyer calls it my zone. I'm just lucky he doesn't refuse to hang with me for being so lame.

"You didn't call," Mom says.

"I forgot."

Out of the corner of my eye, I see her frown.

"We got kinda . . . caught up . . . on a project for school."

"Tell me about it," Mom says.

"We're just . . . filming the neighborhood."

69

"You're being safe? You're not talking to strangers?"

"I'm not Leo . . . remember?"

She shakes her head. "A woman in Allie's building got mugged yesterday. At knifepoint, Joseph."

Allie Klein lives on Fifth Avenue, miles away from here. "So?"

"So, I worry. Two young boys —"

"I'm not going . . . to die." The words exit my mouth by their own power. I stop unloading groceries to check Mom's reaction. She looks like I've just socked her in the teeth. She presses two fingertips to her lips.

"I'm sorry," I say.

She shakes her head. She wets a sponge and starts wiping down the counter even though it's not dirty. "What camera are you using?" Mom asks with forced cheer.

"Huh?"

"For the assign —" Mom turns, but stops mid-sentence when she sees me climbing the step-ladder to put away the cereal boxes. "I'll get that, Joseph."

"It's no problem." I can arrange them by height and color, the way she likes.

"Sweetie, you'll get hurt up there."

"I'm fine." I don't know why Mom even bought cereal. There are three full boxes up here already.

Just as I start to move things around, Mom says urgently, "Joseph, I'll get it!"

I turn to look at her. As I do, my hand knocks two of the cereal boxes to the floor. When I look back at the shelf, I notice that wedged behind them are Hershey's bars. Bags of them. One by one, they slide off the shelf.

Mom and I just look at them and don't say anything.

Suddenly, from the den, we hear Leo screech

71

one of his ambulances to a halt. "Already dead!" he shouts.

Without a word, Mom bends down, picks up the Hershey's bars, and dumps them in the trash. Then she covers her ears with her hands and leaves the room as Leo whines, "No, no, no!"

# "WHEN DAY IS DONE"

After dinner, Mom looks so worn out that I offer to give Leo his bath. I grab the camera and bring it in with me. I film Leo as he pulls off all his clothes and gallops around, yelling, "Nakey, nakey!" He flashes a toothy grin at me and says, "Cheeeeeeese!"

"Brush your teeth," I tell him.

He hops onto his wooden stool that Aunt Jane, Mom's younger sister, made for him when he was born. There's a big picture of a lion on it, along with Leo's name and birth date. You can tell he feels proud of it.

I lay down the camera and run the bathwater. As Leo's brushing (and not very effectively — he sort of sucks the toothbrush instead of moving it

73

across his teeth), I remember Zeke's toothbrush that I left by Jesus' feet.

It disappeared.

Did the homeless girl take that, too?

I'm wondering what other kinds of stuff she needs when Leo hops into the tub and makes a big splash. He almost hits his head on the faucet. I feel a heat crawl up my neck. "Whoa, buddy . . . careful!"

But Leo's not listening. He's suddenly rushing one of his ambulances across the water and making siren noises while I try to wash his hair.

Ms. Conrad's words that Velly read us come floating into my head: "Remember . . . the way your little brother's hair smelled after his bath. . . ." I lean closer to smell Leo. He has sort of a sweet, tangy smell, like a fresh orange slice dipped in vinegar.

Faintly I hear Mom on the phone, and I can tell by the singsongy sound of her voice that it's her sister on the other end. My aunt Jane is very

wait for him to come home from the hospital. I get comfortable on the sofa. The clock reads 9:00, then 10:00, then 11:00, but he never shows.

The next morning, the sky outside my window is gunmetal gray and thick with feeling. I can tell it wants to rain or snow.

The homeless girl pops into my head. I wonder if she sleeps on some slab of dirty cardboard or if she lies awake, waiting for the safety of morning. Could I survive for even one night on the street in the dead of winter?

I toss off the covers, throw on a T-shirt and a pair of sweatpants, and head down the hall to find Dad. I didn't even hear him come in last night, and I want to catch him before he leaves for the hospital. Maybe make some plans to hang, get his advice on the documentary.

But the empty coffee cup in the sink and the

scattered newspaper on the kitchen table tell me that I've already missed him. It's not even eight o'clock.

Between his long hours at the hospital, his volunteer work at a local clinic, and his new obsession with working out, I think the last time I saw him for more than a few minutes was Thanksgiving. That hardly counts because we were at Aunt Jane's with a bunch of her friends. It wasn't like I got to really hang with Dad. And he was on call, so he ended up leaving early.

"There's been a baby boom since September eleventh," Mom offered up gently after he left. She stroked my hair. "That's a good thing, sweetie. Something positive to come from all the devastation."

Maybe so. But why couldn't some other doctor deliver all those babies?

As I'm leaving the kitchen, I see a letter on top of Mom's "To Be Filed" pile. The return address says Rabbi David Dove. I can hear Mom's shower running, so I take a chance and open it.

Dear Lilah,

It was so good to see you last week. I hope what I had to say was helpful. I have seen so many families dissolve when tragedy strikes. Please don't let this happen to yours. As I said, I'd be happy to talk with you and Bob and Joseph anytime.

I am writing now to ask a favor. A new member of our congregation has recently lost a daughter. I wonder if you would be willing to talk to her. . . .

My hands are shaking by the time I finish the letter. Why would Dad and I need to talk to Rabbi David? And what does he mean by "dissolve"? Is Mom thinking of leaving like Flyer's mom? Is Dad? I stuff the letter in the envelope and put it back on the pile. I swallow the hard lump in my throat.

In a daze, I continue down the hall. Quietly, I turn the knob to Zeke's door and go in. I walk to the dresser, open the top drawer, and root around for a pair of wool socks. Zeke always wore them skiing. I find some way in the back of his drawer.

"Yosheph?" I hear.

My heart leaps. Leo is standing in the doorway with his thumb in his mouth and his stuffed lion, Lionel, in a neck lock.

"Wh-what are you doing here?" I don't mean to sound short with him.

"Come play," he whimpers.

I shut the sock drawer and take Leo's hand to lead him out. "I was just borrowing . . . some socks. It's cold out."

"Daddy?" Leo says as I close the door behind us. "Who lives in there?"

so suddenly. But still, coming home right now seems like a long shot.

We cross east on St. Mark's, by the cool Middle Eastern restaurant with the zebra booths. Then down First Avenue and over to Sixth Street so I can film the Indian restaurants where MELLOW SITAR MUSIC FLOATS OUT THE OPEN DOORWAYS, FLYING ME TO BOMBAY AND BANGLADESH.

"Let's eat," Flyer says.

I pat my messenger bag where I've got the wool socks stowed. "Not till we finish our mission."

I walk backwards so I can film Flyer coming toward me. I've got him framed between two trees on either side of the street.

"If you ever become famous, remind me not to work for you," he says.

"If I become famous, remind me that you look better behind the camera . . . than in front of it."

"Ha, ha, ha!" Flyer exhales giant bubbles of laughter, like Melody. He skates toward me, grabs my hat off my head, and whips down the block.

I run after him. I let the camera bob up and down — a technique that was definitely not in my book — and watch the city jump around on my screen until I catch up to Flyer.

He's standing in front of Jesus, with my hat on his head. Spikes of cloud-colored hair poke out from underneath.

"You're a loser," I tell him as I catch my breath.

"I know," he says. "That's why you love me."

I hand him the camera and pull the wool socks out of my bag. I kiss them, then open the glass door and set them by Jesus' feet. Actually, he looks like he could use a pair.

"Merry Christmas," Flyer tells him. "It's almost your birthday, dude. Tell St. Nick to surprise me with something really special this year, okay?"

I gently shut the door and turn to look at Flyer. His eyes are closed. His hands are gripped so tight around the camera and the skateboard that I can see the whites of his knuckles.

"Come on, Fly. Your turn to buy lunch."

Flyer and I are at the counter eating our sandwiches when a cold breeze blows through the café. I look up and see Melody scowling.

The homeless girl has just come in with her dog. They weren't on the sidewalk when we got here.

It's strange seeing the girl beyond her doorway. She is so twiggy, a sharp wind would probably snap her in half. And she walks like a puppet, with stiff, jerky movements. Her head is tucked. She is rubbing her hands up and down her arms.

"The bathroom is for customers only," Melody growls.

Flyer and I exchange a surprised look. Melody never gets mad at anyone.

The girl pauses at the counter. "I'll have a

small coffee, then, black, lots of sugar." Her voice sounds scraped up. She sticks a fist in her cup and dumps the change onto the counter.

"Stay, Jupiter," she tells the dog. He sits down about three feet from me while the girl disappears into the bathroom.

Melody slides the coins into the cash drawer in one angry motion. I watch as she ducks under the counter and starts clearing tables.

What's the big deal about the girl using the bathroom? Is she supposed to pee on the street?

Flyer and I eat in silence. Jupiter inches closer to me and nudges his nose against my pant leg. I lean down to pat his head, and he licks the salt from the potato chips off my fingers.

After a few minutes I whisper, "Do you think she's okay?"

Flyer shrugs. "She's been in there a while."

I guess Melody hears that because she storms over and pounds on the door. "Other people need the bathroom, too!" She sits on the arm of the nearest sofa and waits.

What's up with her? Nobody's in line. What if the girl is sick?

Besides, it's not like anyone would want to hang out in the bathroom. It's a skank pit of graffitti and piss. The old tub is piled to the ceiling with broken computers. The plunger looks like it's been through a war. There's never any soap.

Finally the girl emerges. She's still looking down but doesn't seem wigged out anymore. She isn't rubbing herself.

She slips by Melody and floats to the door without looking up or even taking her coffee. Jupiter trots after her.

Melody ducks back under the counter and

mutters something about installing a blue light in the bathroom.

Flyer and I look at her and say, "Huh?" at the same time.

"Under a blue light," she tells us, "junkies can't find their veins."

# "CHASIN' THE BIRD"

## TEN

We are racing through the park, past Jesus, past the Queen and her dogs, east to Avenue B, beyond my zone.

"Tell me why we're following her," Flyer says as he kicks the pavement to propel himself faster.

When I don't answer, he says, "If the girl just shot junk into her veins, man, you really think she's going to be up for an interview?"

"I just want to see where she goes."

We continue down the block. We leap over potholes. We dodge people and cars, parking signs and fire hydrants.

On our right is a community garden. It's filled with trees and shrubs and, strange as it seems, a few hearty flowers. Flyer motions me inside.

91

There's a mosaic-tiled trellis on the right, picnic tables and benches, and an open-air stage in the back. A couple of people are strolling around.

I turn a full rotation, but I don't see the girl. How could she just vanish?

As I'm turning, I notice a strange wooden structure in the left corner of the garden. It's built from hundreds of crisscrossed beams, reaches about six stories high, and is shaped like a steeple. Balanced on jutting beams and poking out from open spaces are animals — mostly horses — stuffed horses, carousel horses, and soft-sculpture horses. There are also some bears and dogs and a giraffe all the way on top. A big blue toy car, a plastic pumpkin, a teapot, and a tricycle balance alongside the animals. It looks like something right out of *Alice in Wonderland*.

"My dad used to bring me here every Saturday morning," Flyer says. "While he was helping out with the gardens, I'd run around and climb on this thing."

I pull out the camera. I can't believe this has been blocks from my apartment all my life and I never even knew about it. For some reason, that makes me feel mad at Mom.

"A guy from the neighborhood built it in the late eighties. The story goes that he wanted to make it tall enough to watch the nude sunbathers on the rooftops surrounding the garden. This is the second sculpture, actually. My dad and I were here the day the guy tore the first one down. He attached a rope to it and started pulling. I remember people screaming for him to stop because they thought he was going to be crushed. But he just kept pulling and, when the sculpture fell, he went straight through a hole. He didn't even get scraped." Flyer hops off his skateboard to take a closer look. "See the tree he built it around?" Flyer points. "It's amazing it can grow with all that stuff choking it."

I walk closer, too. I find a small opening in the sculpture and push the nose of the camera into it. Fingers of light reach into the dark space. I can make out a dirt floor and a tree root poking up.

I turn as much as I can to film the other side, and suck in a breath.

"What is it, man?"

I move over so Flyer can see what I'm seeing.

"Whoa," he says.

I can tell from the tone of his voice that he's not doubting my theory anymore.

There's a pile of stuff inside — a few old blankets, some clothes, a hat, books, and wool socks — and Flyer knows as well as I do that half of it belonged to Zeke.

"Now what?" Flyer asks. He is skating next to me as we head up the block.

I duck into the nearest deli and start filling a small basket. Cheese, flatbread, bananas, a bottle of juice, tissues, cough drops, and a few candy bars. Flyer follows me around, holding up items for my approval. "Tell me why we're doing this," he says.

HELP ME, HELP ME, HELP ME. PLEASE.

I can't tell Flyer that I think Zeke is trying to communicate with me through his notebook. He'd think I was the weakest dude in the history of man.

"It's Christmas Eve," I say.

"I guess that makes us Santa and his little elf." Flyer lands a soft punch on my arm. Then we go to pay.

The front of the deli sparkles with Christmas lights, the colors of Kwanza, and a menorah, even though Hanukkah was weeks ago. Not that we celebrated or anything.

Flyer nudges me. "Wake up, little elf. It's sixteen dollars."

The woman behind the counter smiles and holds out her hand. "Fifteen dolla, eighty-seven cent."

Flyer throws down a few bills while I dig in my pockets for the rest. Then he grabs the plastic bag and skates out. I follow him. I just hope we'll be able to find an opening in the sculpture big enough to squeeze this stuff through.

# "BACK HOME BLUES"

## ELEVEN

Beethoven's Ninth Symphony is bouncing off the walls of our apartment.

I find Dad in the kitchen. He's conducting an invisible orchestra with his right hand, downing a cup of coffee with his left, and staring out at the trash Dumpster behind our building. I knew his time off would kick in eventually.

He doesn't hear me say hello, so I walk into the den and turn down the stereo.

"Hey, Champ," he says when he sees me. Champ was his nickname for Zeke.

"Hey, Doc."

If Dad notices his mistake, he doesn't let on. He drains his coffee cup and refills it. I lean back awkwardly against the table.

97

When Dad turns to face me again, I notice that his eyes look too wide, as if invisible toothpicks are propping them open. Skin pulled tight around his mouth holds a smile in place. I can see the outline of his bald pate through his thinning hair like the moon through the clouds.

"So —" he starts to say.

"I —" I say at the same time.

"Go ahead," he says.

I notice he's got his scrub pants on. "Boy or . . . girl?" I ask.

"Boy," he says.

"Cool."

Dad yawns. He's only a few feet away, but it feels like we're on opposite sides of the Grand Canyon. Like if I reach for him I'm going to drop into this dark, gaping chasm.

"Where are Mom and Leo?"

Dad pinches the bridge of his nose. "The library. Or maybe with Janey. What day is it?"

"Tuesday. Flyer and his dad . . . invited me . . . for Christmas Eve dinner. I'd be . . . home early."

"It's fine with me, but you'd better ask your mother when she gets back," Dad says. "I'll be at the hospital."

"Didn't you just . . . come from . . . there?"

"I've got twins tonight."

I nod.

I remember when we used to eat dinner together every night. Some nights, while Mom was going for her PhD and writing her dissertation, it was just us guys. Dad would tell me stories about his childhood in Brooklyn while I helped him make the salad or set the table. There was one story about breaking a window while playing stickball, another about riding his bike along the boardwalk in Brighton Beach with Grandpa Harry, and another about delivering groceries for Zingerman's Market when Grandpa Harry died. I loved hearing Dad talk.

A memory flashes in my head. Dad is tickling me on the living room floor until I am breathless with laughter. He digs into his satchel, pulls out a stethoscope, and holds it to my elbow. Then he makes a sober face. "This is serious, kid. You've got Ticklitis — inflammation of the funny bones. I think we're going to have to amputate. Hold on a minute while I go get my chain saw."

Dad coughs and glances out the window again.

There's a knot of quiet in the kitchen. The refrigerator hums. The ice maker gurgles. The coffeemaker clicks itself off.

I think about what Flyer said this afternoon. That I should just come right out and ask what's on my mind. But it's not like I haven't tried.

Back in September I did.

I guess Mom and Dad forgot to notify Yale about Zeke because two months after he died, the day before I started eighth grade, someone from admissions called asking why he hadn't matriculated or something.

Mom had stopped answering the phone back then. It was all she could do to get dressed and take care of Leo and remember to order us takeout for dinner.

We'd barely seen Dad in the two months since Zeke had died, except coming and going and the bunch of times I'd found him asleep in front of the TV in the middle of the night when I couldn't sleep. You'd think he would have thought to call Yale, since it was his alma mater, but I was the one who had to tell them that Zeke wouldn't be coming to their school because he was dead.

That was the first time I felt the words lagging in my throat, collapsing in my mouth.

Dad was sitting on the sofa when I went to talk to him. He was looking in my direction. But his face was the color of putty, and his eyes were vacant. I asked him about the phone call, if I'd said the right thing, because I knew Mom's rule about family business staying in the family. He just nodded absently.

I wanted to ask him other stuff — if he was mad at me for sleeping over at Flyer's on the Fourth of July, and if Zeke knew what he was doing when he drank half a bottle of vodka — but the words just crumbled on my tongue, and after a while, Dad rubbed his eyes and said, "I'm sorry, Joseph, but I don't feel like talking anymore."

He stared at me blankly for another few seconds before turning back to the news on TV.

"Joseph?" Dad asks now. "Were you going to say something?"

I notice my mouth is open. "I'm making . . . a documentary . . . for school."

"On what?" he asks.

"The neighborhood. Velly said —"

"Sounds interesting." Dad sips his coffee.

"Maybe you . . . could help me . . . with it?"

"Hmmm. Tomorrow might work," he says.

"Sure." I smile. "Who knows . . . I could be . . . the next . . . Ken Burns."

"That's certainly a goal." He reaches over and tousles my hair. He throws back the last sip of coffee and sets the cup in the sink. I can tell he's about to bolt.

"I met this . . . girl, Dad. I think . . . Zeke . . . knew her."

His lips fold inward and touch his teeth. He checks his watch. "Whoa. I'll see you later. I've got to run."

Before I can even get out my next sentence, he is gone.

# TWELVE

# "WHITE CHRISTMAS"

The doorman buzzes me up to Flyer's. Mr. Gray pokes his head into the hallway to greet me. He's wearing a plaid apron over a green wool sweater. His hair is the color of asphalt. His eyes are small and squinty. They make him look like he's smiling through his wire-rimmed glasses even when he isn't.

"Hey, Jed! Merry Christmas, happy almost-Kwanza." Mr. Gray wraps me in a big bear hug and squeezes around my shoulders. My body collapses into the memory of that feeling. My eyes start to well up, which is so stupid.

He guides me into the apartment and shuts the door. "Give me your coat."

I shake it off and blink back the tears.

"You okay?"

"Sure," I manage. "Just . . . the cold."

"I made some hot cider. Come on, I'll have some with you. T, Jed is here!"

I follow Mr. Gray through the living room, which opens up into the kitchen. An overstuffed sofa and chair sit on a thick warm carpet. Books and papers and stacks of unopened mail clutter every surface.

It smells amazing, like ginger and garlic and cinnamon. The table is set with a red velvet cloth, mini gingerbread houses in front of every plate, and wooden candlesticks that Mr. Gray carved. He's missing half of his right pinkie from a wood-working accident.

There are four place settings. Which means either Mr. Gray got a girlfriend within the past several hours, or Flyer has been hiding a friend worthy of Christmas Eve dinner (not), or he thinks there's still a chance his mom might show up.

105

It kills me, but I vote for number three.

Mr. Gray hands me a mug of cider and raises his own mug. "To an easier year for you, Jed."

I raise my glass, too. "Thanks, Mr. Gray."

"To a better year for all of us."

We are both about to take a sip when Mr. Gray looks up. Flyer's Cheshire Cat grin spreads across his face.

Flyer has just swaggered into the room. His hair is pink. And not just any pink. We're talking Coney Island cotton candy.

"And to change!" Mr. Gray lifts his mug again. "Cheers, T. It looks great." He holds out a mug for Flyer. "You guys want to put on some music?"

Flyer takes the cider without acknowledging Mr. Gray's compliment.

We knock fists and say, "Whazzup?" at the same time.

"You like it?" he asks.

"It's bold."

Flyer struts across the room over to the stereo. "Pink is Mom's favorite color." He pops in a CD of Christmas carols.

Shoot, he is really gone.

In a few minutes, we sit down to dinner at the small square table: me, Flyer, Mr. Gray, and the uninvited guest. It's painful to look at the empty place setting, and worse to watch Flyer fill its glass with wine. But Mr. Gray doesn't say a word. He just clasps his hands together, closes his eyes, and bows his head. Flyer does the same, so I follow.

"I feel grateful for this abundant meal and this abundantly good company. In the coming year, may all beings, everywhere, be happy and free, and may the thoughts and actions of our lives contribute to that happiness and to that freedom for all. Amen."

"Amen," Flyer and I echo together.

"Dad's going all Buddhist on me," Flyer says jokingly. "It's the religion du jour."

Mr. Gray laughs. "That was a yogic mantra."

"Of course, the Christmas Eve yogurt prayer." Flyer smirks as we pass around Mr. Gray's feast. He and Flyer are vegetarians, so there are tofu steaks, sweet potato mash, grilled vegetables, white beans, and homemade rolls. It sounds weird, but it's good.

"Did you and your family do anything special for Hanukkah?" Mr. Gray asks.

"Oh, we don't celebrate anymore."

Mr. Gray gives me a puzzled look.

"Don't pry, Dad. Dr. Diamond doesn't believe in religion anymore, okay?"

Mr. Gray looks concerned. "Theo told me about your bar mitzvah, but I figured you'd just reschedule in due time."

I shake my head.

"Because of Zeke?" Mr. Gray asks.

"Dad, just leave it alone." Flyer's voice is edged.

"It's okay," I say. I like Mr. Gray's questions. And my words don't jam so much when I talk to him.

"I'm really sorry, Jed." Mr. Gray pauses and takes a bite of potatoes. "It's funny how people blame God when bad things happen. I'm not claiming to have the answers myself. Believe me, Theo and I have struggled these past months to understand the upheaval in our lives. We're still struggling."

Flyer gives his dad a dark look.

Mr. Gray looks back at him thoughtfully. "I think a lot of people get hung up because they think God is supposed to be the great problem solver, and they lose faith when He or She doesn't magically lift their burdens."

I put my fork down and listen.

"Can I tell you a story from India?" Mr. Gray asks.

Flyer groans, but Mr. Gray ignores him when I nod.

"In a land not so far away, in a time not so long ago, people were always nagging God. Some asked to be healed, others to be married, others to have more children or land or wealth. God would try to hide. But wherever He hid, the people always found Him and continued with their selfish requests. They were always dissatisfied.

"One day, God called together a counsel of other gods and goddesses at Mount Meru, seeking advice. Shiva suggested He hide on the moon, but God was sure the people would find Him there. Vishnu told Him to hide at the bottom of the ocean, but God knew that wouldn't work, either. Finally, Sarasvati laughed. 'The solution is obvious. Hide inside their own hearts. That is the last place they would ever think to look.'"

Flyer is staring down at his plate, shoveling food into his mouth. I can tell he's annoyed. It could be that he's heard that story a thousand times, but I'm guessing he's finally figuring out that his mom is a no-show.

"My own search for God has been long and difficult," Mr. Gray goes on. "It's what led me to study world religions. I guess you could say I'm on a journey. I try to stay patient with myself because my ideas are changing all the time, especially since September eleventh. How do you reconcile something like that? How do you believe that a loving God would allow something so heinous to happen?" Mr. Gray frowns and sips his red wine.

I've asked myself that a hundred times. Why all those innocent people? Why Zeke?

"What do you think . . . now?" I ask.

"I think we are responsible for the things we can control," Mr. Gray continues, "like what kind of person we want to be, and what path we want our life to take. But the things we can't control, like terrorism and your brother's death and Mrs.

Gray's leaving," he says, looking first at me and then at Flyer, "we just have to do the best we can to accept them. And try to find the things we're supposed to learn from them. Some of our greatest thinkers have said that it's the tragedies that shape our lives, and the deeper our sorrow, the greater our capacity for joy. In other words, sometimes a blessing can emerge from misfortune." Mr. Gray sips his wine pensively while Flyer broods.

I'm not sure if they're connected or not, but Mr. Gray's words remind me of something Rabbi David said at Zeke's funeral. "Those who live a long life see the fruits of their labors. But for those whose lives are cut short, others benefit from them. Ezekiel Diamond touched many people profoundly in his brief time on Earth. He will live on in the memories of those people and all the people who loved him. May his memory be a blessing."

Those words sounded good, but still . . . I don't know what kind of blessing it is or what you're supposed to learn from someone dying before he even learned to drive.

"Jed didn't come here for a lecture," Flyer says tightly. "You know, you really know how to ruin a holiday." He pushes back his chair, stands, and leaves.

An awkward silence fills the room.

"I'm sorry, Jed. I guess I can get carried away sometimes."

"I like hearing what you have to say."

"Thanks. I guess that's more than I can say for my own son right now."

I shake my head. "He's just sore because . . ."

Mr. Gray nods and stares at the empty place setting. "Please keep eating. I'll be right back." He stands and steps around the corner. I hear him knock on Flyer's door and then open it. I can't really make out what he says, but I do hear the words "I'm sorry," and "Will you join us?"

I guess Flyer says no, because in a minute, Mr. Gray returns by himself.

He sits back down. He looks upset. "I don't think Theo's really up to socializing tonight. Why don't I walk you home."

I nod. "I'll just go say good-bye."

When I open Flyer's door, he's at the computer. I can see part of the screen. It looks like he's on cheaptickets.com, checking out flights.

"Your dad is walking me home. You want to come?"

Flyer shakes his head.

"You leave for Maine tomorrow, right? For a week?"

Flyer nods.

"That sucks. We didn't even finish the documentary."

Flyer leans over and grabs the camera off his desk. He holds it out to me.

"I could try to finish while you're gone," I say.

He shakes his head. "The camera's yours, dude. I'm giving it to you. And the documentary is yours, too. You've done all the work. I'm not even that good with the camera. I'll come up with something else for the assignment. Here, take it." He pushes the camera toward me.

"Fly, I can't —"

"You'll use it more than I will. Besides, I don't want it anymore."

I take the camera. "Thanks," I say.

"Merry Christmas, dude."

"Call me when you're back."

Flyer and I knock fists. Then I shut his door and leave the building with Mr. Gray.

The streets are hushed. A thin, white blanket has covered the sidewalks. As we walk, Mr. Gray holds up his right hand and wriggles his fingers. "When it snows," he says, "I can feel my whole pinkie, even the tip that's missing."

"That's cool." I laugh.

"It's called a phantom limb. Some people who've lost parts of themselves say the sensation is a torment. But I disagree. I like remembering what that little guy felt like."

Mr. Gray throws an arm around my shoulder, and we walk the rest of the way in silence. Snow is still coming down. The wind lifts and swirls it around us.

When we round the corner on East Tenth Street, I look up and see our water tower, A GLIMMER IN THE MIDST OF WOE . . . A FRIEND TO THOSE WHO SEEK YOU. . . .

And just for that moment, like a phantom limb, I feel Zeke's nearness.

# "TEMPTATION"

## THIRTEEN

Mom and Dad's door is still shut when I wake up the next morning. Dad's probably sleeping in after a long night at the hospital. I'm excited to show him the footage I've shot so far, and to ask his advice on what to do now that Flyer will be gone for the rest of vacation.

I wander into the kitchen, toast a bagel, and bring it into the den to eat.

Leo is watching Clifford. I grab the clicker and channel surf.

"Yoseph, no!" Leo wails.

"Come on, Leo. I want to watch TV."

"Clifford," Leo whines, and starts to cry.

I ignore him and keep surfing. I stop when I get to a documentary on some cable-access

117

station. It's about the water towers in New York City.

Leo runs out of the room, yelling, "Mommy!"

A ten-year-old kid is reporting:

"There are about ten thousand water towers dotting New York City's skyline. Did you know that every building over six stories high needs one on its rooftop in order to get decent water pressure? The towers are designed to hold enough water for one day's usage, before refilling at night. They are made from a heavy yellow cedar, which resists temperature changes and corrosion. And they are constructed for the first time right on top of the buildings."

The kid takes us to the site of a newly built tower, which is just getting filled. When the workmen hear the water rush up, they give a mighty shout.

The kid brings the mike over to one of the

men and asks him to describe what it's like working up here.

"The tanks come in pieces, you know, and all the work is done by hand. It can be a pretty gruelin' job, and dangerous, too. You could fall four feet or the whole height of the building if you're not careful.

"And in the summer, it's hotter than *bleep* up here. Sometimes we swim around in the tanks. Stuff can get caught in them, too. One tenant I heard about had bird feathers comin' out of his faucet.

"But every day you see somethin' new up on the roofs of New York — people eatin' lunch, makin' commercials, once I even seen a wedding. These towers are a symbol of the city. I feel proud to be a part a that."

The kid returns the mike to his own mouth. "If you have a water tower on top of your build-

119

ing, now you'll know how it works, and you'll probably never look at it the same way again.

"For *New York Kids,* this is Jason Nair reporting live from Union Square in New York City."

When Mom comes into the room, holding Leo, I ask her why we need a water tower on our building when we're only six stories high.

"That tank hasn't functioned for years. Don't you remember when the co-op board thought about tearing it down? Dad and I fought to keep it."

I shake my head.

"I guess you were little. Anyway, we were lucky most of the tenants agreed that it would be a shame to lose something that is so quintessentially New York."

I pick up my bagel off the coffee table and take a bite.

"Will you come? Janey and Violet are meeting us." Mom's not looking at me. She's watching the crumbs fall on my lap and on the sofa. I can feel how badly she wants to run and get the vacuum cleaner.

"I'm waiting for Dad . . . to get up. He's helping . . . with my documentary."

Mom frowns. "Dad's at the hospital, honey."

She must see the disappointment on my face because she manufactures a smile and says, "Babies don't know it's a holiday," and then, "Why don't you come with us?" She says this last part as if battling the tourists in Midtown just to see some stupid tree and some stupid holiday windows, which I'm too old for anyway, should console me.

I shake my head. "I have to meet Flyer," I lie.

"Jade Mountain at five, then."

"I know." We eat dinner there every Christmas. Same time, same channel.

"He said he'd make it for dinner," Mom says, repositioning Leo on her hip.

I nod, still staring at the TV.

"Okay, Joseph. Five o'clock."

"I heard you . . . the first . . . time."

"Please clean up after yourself."

I accidentally spill my plate of crumbs to the floor.

Finally, they leave.

# "YARDBIRD SUITE"

## FOURTEEN

When I'm certain Mom and Leo are long gone, I throw on my jacket, grab the camera, and fly up three flights of stairs. You never know who will see you exit the elevator on the wrong floor and get suspicious.

At the top of the stairs there's another smaller set of stairs leading to a big steel door. Quietly, I push it open and step out into the cold air. The snow has melted, and my boots crunch the black tar roof. Clouds smoke out of my mouth.

Time seems suspended up here. Car alarms and fire engines and taxi horns lose their edge by the time they reach me. And the world below has turned itself into a play set I could maneuver like Legos.

123

Why did I ever listen to Zeke and stop coming up here? Even though we're not that high, the views are spectacular. To the east is the East River; to the north, the gleaming spire of the Empire State Building. To the west are the zigzag streets of the West Village; and to the south, the mighty Brooklyn Bridge and the wound in our skyline where the Twin Towers were.

Around me, in every direction, is a forest of water towers.

It's funny how a bunch of the newer buildings try to hide their towers inside huge brick squares and circles, as if they're something to be ashamed of. But the tower heads stretch up above the brick walls rebelliously, shouting out a big "Huzzah!" to the city.

Beside me, our tower rises toward the clouds like a mighty rocket, mammoth and fierce. As I make a circle to film it, a grayish-brown blur flies across my screen. I look up and see the biggest bird I have ever seen. It reminds me of the giant bird I saw the day Flyer and I started the documentary.

The bird overhead has broad wings, a fanned tail, and a brown band of color around its belly. It's a hawk, I think.

The bird hovers and then lands on the tip of the tower. It doesn't seem afraid. Call me crazy, but it seems to pose for the camera, cocking its head one way and then another as I film it.

"Hey bird, you forget to migrate or something?"

Maybe the bird understands. Maybe it thinks, Oh, yeah, good idea, dude, because after a few more seconds, it lifts off into the sky. It flies toward me at first. The pale feathers near its wing tips look like headlights aiming straight for my eyes. I duck, even though the bird isn't low enough to hit me, and then I crane my neck to watch it fly up and east and away.

The nose of the camera is still aimed at the tower's pointy cap, and slowly, I angle my shot down the weathered wooden body to the black steel legs all the way to the roof. I film the ladder running from bottom to top.

Without even thinking, I wiggle the camera strap onto my wrist and start climbing. The wind kicks up. It whips my hair and inflates my jacket. There is a sense of lightness up here, and for a moment I feel like I could lift off like that bird, like the *milagro* around my neck.

When I reach the base of the tank, I notice a metal latch.

I look closer. I touch it. It's a door latch. It's holding shut a crudely cut door, carved into the tower.

That's weird. The documentary didn't say anything about doors.

It did say that the towers are designed to hold

one day's worth of water. If this one hasn't been used for years, does that mean it's empty?

Maybe rotten water will spill all over me, maybe I'll fall backwards. . . .

I unhook the latch and push the door open. Nothing comes at me except a musky smell. It's dark inside, like a cave, but dry.

I step inside. I hold the door open a crack to let in some light. That's when I feel my foot kick something. My heart jumps. *Oh, man. Please don't let it be a rat.*

But then I hear a rolling sound. I grope around and finally put my hand on the thing. It's cold and shaped like a sausage link or a fat Magic Marker, but much heavier. I realize it's a flashlight. I turn the head, and a weak light flickers on and off. It's just enough to illuminate a few feet in front of me.

The space is about as big as half a bus, only round. The roof is peaked. The wooden floor planks creak and groan when I walk. I drag my fingers along the walls, which are as smooth and dry as a table. "He-llo," I say softly. My voice hollows out, the way it used to sound when Zeke and I called to each other through walkie-talkies we had made from empty toilet paper rolls.

The hushed darkness reminds me of the forts we used to build in his bedroom. I could have spent all afternoon in there, the two of us pretending to be pirates on a bounty ship, or captains on a whaling adventure, or soldiers in the bush. But after an hour or so, Zeke would usually kick me out. If I suggested we build a fort while he had a friend over, he'd look at me like he had no idea what I was talking about and would tell me forts were for babies. Then he'd yell for Mom to come get rid of me, which she always did.

What was so wrong with me that I couldn't stay?

When I've made almost a full circle, my foot lands on something soft. I aim the flashlight down at my feet. I'm standing on a thin, woven rug. There are pillows on it, as well as a blanket. I bend down to touch them. The pillowcases are soft and cold. The blanket is made of scratchy wool. It's too dark to make out colors and patterns.

I suddenly place the smell in here. Incense. Patchouli.

I don't even feel my knees buckle, but the next thing I know, I am sitting on the blanket.

Is this Zeke's stuff? Is that why he was climbing the ladder and telling Flyer and me to get lost?

A prickle of heat crawls into my chest, then spreads out over my whole body.

*When did he come here why didn't he ever tell me what did he do up here who was he trying to get away from was it me?*

I fall back onto one of the pillows. It holds a

faint smell of patchouli. Next to it, I find a few burnt incense cones on a scrap of tinfoil. I pick one up. It crumbles to dust in my fingers.

I hug the pillow. Hard. Then harder. And before I know it, I am standing up and thrashing it against the walls.

*Why did you leave didn't you love us you were going to take me traveling remember I would never have bailed on you.*

"I hate you I hate you I hate you!" I shout as the pillow explodes in a blizzard of feathers.

# "PERDIDO"

I need air. I start walking, I don't even know
where to. As I'm crossing Tenth Street, a taxi
swerves around me and skids on black ice. The
driver lays on his horn and shakes a fist at me. He
rolls down his window and yells something I can't
understand.

I keep walking.

Most of the places along Avenue A are closed
up. A bunch of winos are stumbling around.

Up ahead, a guy with a knit Rasta cap and a
drum slung across his back is bopping down the
street. Jamal! I speed up. As I'm stepping off the
curb, my foot lands in a puddle of slush. I get wet
up to my ankles. When I finally reach the guy, he
turns to me. He's got hooded eyes and freckles, a

131

face too thin and cruel to be Jamal's. He shoots me a look and asks if I've got a problem.

I turn back around.

I end up by Jesus. I must be out of my head because his wounds look bigger today. They seem to bloat and ooze.

A bad-looking dude comes up and asks me for money. Tells me he needs a dollar fifty for a subway token, to get to his job uptown.

"Sorry," I mumble, and walk away.

I can feel him following me. Not a soul on the street. My heart starts to race. I break into a run.

Finally I duck into the café.

"What's up, Frog?" Melody says.

We both check the door.

"Nothing." I hop onto a stool. I try not to let it show that I'm sucking air.

"You want some hot chocolate? On the house today."

132

I nod.

She smiles at the guy sitting next to me. "I'll be right back."

I turn to check him out. He's got thick, wavy hair, horn-rimmed glasses, and a jaw like Superman. A crossword puzzle sits on the counter in front of him, and between him and me, a pack of Marlboro Reds. The dude lifts his big chin in my direction to acknowledge me.

"T'sup?" I say, and turn away.

Melody squeezes his hand as she passes him. Then she sets down my drink in front of me. "So is it time for my interview?" She laughs.

I'm not in the mood.

Melody picks up the camera. She trains the lens on me. "How 'bout I interview you, Jed?"

I open my mouth to say no, but nothing comes out.

"Tell me something about yourself."

I reach for the camera, but Melody pulls away

and keeps shooting. "What's the most defining thing that's ever happened to you?" she asks.

"Cut it out!" The words come out louder than I intend.

Superman turns to glare at me. Melody moves the camera away from her face. "Are you okay, Frog?"

"Give me the camera," I croak, my voice like a pathetic amphibian imitation.

She hands it to me. "I was just trying to have a little fun."

"Yeah, well . . . maybe some other time." I know Melody doesn't know about Zeke, but still.

I hop off my stool and duck into the bathroom to splash cold water on my face. When I come out, Melody is leaning over the counter, reading crossword clues upside down.

As I pass her and the guy, I slide his smokes off the counter and into my pocket. They're so into their stupid crossword puzzle, they don't even notice.

I cross the park. Two plastic bags sprung from the trash float by on the wind, like ghosts. A man and his son are shooting hoops. At the other end of the court, a bunch of guys are skateboarding. They don't have half the moves Flyer has.

I pass the dog run and see the Queen exit the gate with her posse. She smiles. "Merry Christmas, love."

A hard ball clumps in my throat, but I manage to cough out, "I'm . . . Jewish."

She starts making apologies, but I am already gone. I'm such a jerk.

I head farther east and south. I don't stop until I reach the city garden. There's no one inside today. I go in and sit on the edge of the small stage. Except for an occasional bus going by and the faint beat of salsa music falling from someone's apartment window, it is strangely quiet in here.

I pull out the smokes and lift the cardboard top. There's a book of matches inside. I pop a cigarette in my mouth and light it. I take a drag and suck it down. Suddenly I get a head rush, and my whole chest feels like it's going to explode. I open my mouth to let out the smoke and hack like a fiend, like I might cough up a lung.

So many thoughts are crowding my brain, it feels like my head is going to burst. To steady myself, I try to focus on the tip of the cigarette. It's a perfectly round red ember. I touch it to the palm of my left hand for a second. I hear the hiss of burning skin. A rod of pain shoots through my hand and up my arm.

I drop the cigarette and grind it out with my boot, then ditch the rest of the pack in the trash can behind me. I cup my head in my hands and try to make the world stop spinning.

"What do you have to cry about?"

Big gray eyes, flat and unblinking, stare down at me.

"What's a matter? Cat got your tongue?" The girl's hands dig into her sweatshirt pockets. Her bony arms stick out like kite wings.

"I'm not crying."

"Your cheek is wet."

I wipe it with the back of my hand.

"Tears make me nervous." She sits down next to me. Her skin is so pale, it's almost translucent. Her lips are as red as apples. There is something otherworldly about her.

"You shouldn't smoke," she says. "It'll kill you."

The dog, Jupiter, licks my knee. I pat his head, and he nudges his snout into my crotch.

"Quit it, Jupe," the girl says. "He's a bit of a pervert."

Jupiter rests his chin on my knee. I scratch behind his ears.

The girl swings her feet out and back, making a hard, rhythmic thump on the stage. She pulls a comb from her back pocket and drags it through her hair.

I nod toward the sculpture. "Do you live in there?"

"Jupiter loves bananas."

I watch her comb her hair. My words don't seem to be freezing up so much. "Did you know Zeke?"

"I don't beg, guy. I accept donations for my cause, but it isn't begging."

I nod. It's strange how this girl answers and doesn't answer all at once. "That's his comb."

"And I don't take drugs. You think I want to mess myself up with that junk?"

In my head, I picture Melody freaking out about this girl. But for some reason, I believe what she says. "I didn't say —"

"Freedom is everyone's right, yeah, guy?"

138

The girl rests the comb on her leg. "Jupe and me, we're makin' a national tour. Statue of Liberty, Independence Hall and Liberty Bell in Philadelphia, Freedom Trail in Boston. We're carvin' our own freedom trail, right, Jupe?"

Jupiter lets out a low moan.

The girl drums the fingers of her right hand on her left elbow. She's stopped kicking, and now her knees are shimmying up and down. "You like to read?"

"Poetry," I say. "The books are Zeke's."

"You can't believe the stuff people toss. Hardbacks — in the trash!"

"Not the trash. By Jesus. I put them there. Five or so."

"I like thrillers, the darker and gorier the better. Don't say that number." She shivers. "Unlucky number."

The girl starts doing that weird rubbing thing she was doing in the café. Both hands go up and

139

down her arms in a panicky motion. Maybe she's just cold, but I don't think that's it.

"I'm thinkin' about writin' some stories. Sellin' 'em to magazines, maybe. We're gonna see lotsa stuff on our travels."

"Do you have places to stay?"

"My peeps don't care. They don't even know."

"Know what?"

The girl hops off the stage and gives a quick whistle for Jupiter. She turns and heads toward the street in her strange colt-like gait. "See you round, Jed," she calls back.

She is out the gate and around the corner before I even realize I never told her my name.

# "BLUES #2"

## SIXTEEN

"Hey, it's the J-man. How are you, honey?" Aunt Jane reaches out an arm to embrace me as I approach their table at Jade Mountain.

Mom is seated across from Aunt Jane, with Violet and Leo in booster seats on either side of them.

"Do you want to order for the table?" Aunt Jane hands me a menu as I sit down between her and Leo.

Our waiter comes over and sets down a bowl of fried noodles.

Mom says cheerily, "You should have seen the windows at Saks, Joseph —"

"Where's Dad?"

"He's still at the hospital."

"You said . . . he was coming."

Mom sighs. "Honey, he can't predict what's going to happen during delivery."

"Why isn't he here? He's *never* here!"

Mom's eyes dart to the tables around us. A few people look over. One woman is downright staring. Mom smiles weakly. "There were some complica —"

"Are you splitting up?"

"Joseph! Where would you get an idea like that?"

Aunt Jane puts a hand on my shoulder and squeezes.

"I'm not hungry," I say, getting up.

"Joseph, please sit down," Mom says. I can see a vein pulsing in her temple.

"Why? So we can pretend we're a normal family?"

"This isn't the place — you're being rude," she says softly.

"S'cuse you, Yoseph!" Leo pipes up.

"Do you want to get some air, Joey?" Aunt Jane asks.

More people are looking at us now, like we're an episode of *Jerry Springer*.

I grab my coat and head for the door. I hear the staring woman say to her friend, "God, I'm so glad my adolescence is over."

As I pass her table, I say, "Yeah, long over."

My head is pounding by the time I sit down on the bench outside the restaurant. It's snowing again. I open my left hand to check the burn mark. It's blistered now. I don't even realize I'm picking at it until pus oozes onto my palm. The wind bites into my cheeks and freezes my hands and feet. But I just sit there and let myself grow numb.

At last, Mom and Leo come out. We walk home in silence. Leo falls asleep in his stroller. Mom pushes fast, maneuvering along the snowy sidewalk. Some

143

of the brownstones are decorated with wreaths and garlands and white lights.

I hear Mom take a breath. "I know you're hurting, Joseph. I'm sorry. Your father and I, well, we're all trying to cope as best we can. Sometimes we fail, but it doesn't mean we give up on one another."

The lights on one of the houses blink on and off.

"Janey thinks you don't tell us what's going on inside you because you don't want to hurt us or make waves. Is that true?"

I shrug.

"I don't want to lose you, Joseph. But you're so quiet. Sometimes I think I've already lost you."

"Dad's the one . . . who's AWOL."

"We've lost so much," Mom says softly. "We're never going to be the same family we were, but we've got to find a way to hold on to what we have left."

The bells at the church down the street begin to toll, a low, dark sound, like a warning.

A few minutes later, we round the corner onto our block. Someone is sitting on the steps of our building, huddled against the cold. The person's head pops up as we approach. It's about thirty degrees, but I feel my neck get hot.

Mom and I are just about to lift Leo's stroller up the short flight of steps when Mom stops. "Are you okay?" she asks.

The girl nods and strokes her dog. "Just waitin' for a friend."

"Well, I hope she doesn't keep you waiting long," Mom says. "It's frigid out here."

"He'll be right down." The girl's eyes lock into mine.

A raw, nervous feeling worms through my chest. We climb the stairs, and Mom puts her key in the door.

The girl gets up and follows us inside.

I can't believe this is happening.

When Mom notices, the girl says, "I think I'll wait for him in the lobby. Warmer."

Mom gives her a once-over. I wait for her to ask the girl her friend's name. To my surprise, she just says, "Good night."

I watch her head down the hallway. I hear the elevator doors open. I stare at the girl, sitting on a chair next to a small Christmas tree.

"Joseph?" Mom calls.

The girl seems so small, so frail. Her eyes *are* haunting. "Hope your friend shows," I say.

She strokes Jupiter and pulls dirt off his fur.

"Good night," I say.

She doesn't answer.

Finally, I turn and go to Mom.


In my room, I try to distract myself with the film footage I loaded onto my computer a couple of days ago. When that doesn't work, I slip in a Charlie Parker CD and play Tank Hunter.

What is the girl doing down there?

What am *I* doing? She must be SOMEONE'S SISTER . . . DAUGHTER, FRIEND. . . . There must be a reason she found me.

Man, I wish Flyer was around. He'd tell me if I'm losing my mind.

I've just destroyed an enemy tank when Mom pops her head in. "I'm exhausted, honey. I'm going to bed. You need anything?"

"No."

"Okay, good night, then."

"Good night."

I play another round. I go into the den and flip on the TV. I wait till I'm sure Mom is asleep. Then I tiptoe down the hall, slip on my coat and shoes, and, as silently as a cat, slink out the door.

**SEVENTEEN**

# "BIRD FEATHERS"

The chair in the lobby is empty. I trace a path through the small space, even though all of it is in plain view. I peer out the glass doors. Snow is falling harder now. The wind blows in brutal gusts.

"Glad I'm not out there."

I spin around.

The girl is standing behind me, holding a *Vogue* magazine. She must have dug it out of the recycle bin around the corner. Jupiter is by her side, with his tongue hanging out the side of his mouth.

"Your mom's cool."

"How did you know where I live?"

"I followed you." She says this as if stalking people is a normal thing to do.

I guess I shouldn't talk.

148

"How do you know my name?"

She shrugs. "Your friend talks loud." She starts rolling the magazine like it's a wet washcloth she's trying to wring dry. "I'm not homeless, guy."

"I only have five minutes."

The girl looks like she's seen a ghost. "Don't say that number. Bad sign. I should go."

"Wait."

We stare at each other. The hardness of her gaze has melted into two soft orbs, like twin full moons.

I can't bring her upstairs, Mom would freak. I can't sneak her into Zeke's room. What about the dog? I guess she could sleep in the lobby. But what if someone finds her? They'll kick her out or call the cops.

Suddenly the answer rings out as loud and clear as Charlie's sax.

I lead the girl and Jupiter to the elevator. In a minute, we are exiting on the top floor, pushing through the steel door at the top of the stairs.

On the roof, the wind kicks up. The girl is knocked sideways a few steps. She lets out a little scream. "Where are we going?"

"Shhh." I grab her hand. It's tiny and cold. I can feel every bone. When we reach the base of the water tower, I motion for her to start climbing.

Her face turns wary. She backs away.

"You can sleep up there."

I can see she's afraid. Of heights, maybe. Of me.

"I won't hurt you. I'll spot you."

I walk toward her. Her eyes go wide. Gently, I reach out my hand to hers.

She takes another step back.

I inch closer. "Please," I say.

The wind cuts into our skin.

Finally she takes my hand.

Jupiter whines when he sees the girl on the ladder. I grab him around the middle, cradle him under my right arm. Thankfully, he only weighs about twenty-five pounds, a little less than Leo. It's dicey with the wind and only one free hand, but I manage.

Once we're inside, I put Jupiter down and grope for the flashlight. The bulb is even weaker now, but it gives just enough light to reveal the space. Jupiter sniffs nervously.

The wind smacks the wooden structure. The girl takes the flashlight from me. She aims it in a ring. "This thing's not gonna blow over, is it?"

I shake my head.

The girl looks around. She rubs her arms. She rocks back and forth on her boots. "Did a bird die in here or something?"

I look at the pile of feathers. I bend down and try to stuff them back into the pillow.

"Whose stuff is this?" she asks.

"It used to be my brother's. He's dead now."

The girl stops rubbing and rocking. "Sorry."

I look at my watch. I've been gone way more than five minutes.

The girl folds her legs on top of the blanket. Jupiter trots over and sits next to her. "You hang out here a lot?"

I am squatting in front of them, trying to plug the hole in the pillow with the edge of the case. I shake my head. "I just found it."

The girl hugs her knees and looks around the dimly lit space.

"I'll come back tomorrow," I tell her.

She scratches behind Jupiter's ears. She kisses the top of his head. "I lost my whole family," she says.

I stop what I'm doing and look at her. "How?"

She shakes her head.

Without thinking, I lean over and hug her around the shoulders.

"Kiki," she whispers.

I let her go and sit back on my heels.

"That's my name."

Kiki. It sounds like a bird's call, like a song Charlie might play. I reach into my jacket and touch the *milagro* around my neck.

"Good night, Kiki," I say. And then I head back into the storm.

# EIGHTEEN

## "CRAZEOLOGY"

I am at the Central Park Zoo, chewing a fat wad of gum. Overhead, an airplane is churning through the sky. I hear it, but can't see it. I blow a bubble, bigger than my face. I smile at my skill, then suck the bubble back into my mouth to pop it. The gum coats my throat. It covers my windpipe. When I try to inhale, I pull gum into my lungs, instead of air. Suddenly, everything starts to shrink and close in around me. I clutch my throat. I feel my eyes go wide. That's when I realize I'm in my bed, sweating and gasping for breath. I poke around in my mouth for the gum, but there is only the thick, milky paste of morning. And the sound, the coffee grinder, whirling in the kitchen.

I lie there for a while, watching my chest go

up and down. If I stop *thinking* about breathing, will I stop breathing? And why was I dreaming about being at the zoo? I hate zoos.

As I scroll back through the dream, I realize that Zeke was there. He was sitting on a bench, eating ice cream. When he saw my enormous bubble, he'd given me the thumbs up.

I lie in bed for a while, until I'm breathing normally again. Then I toss off the covers and follow the heady smell of freshly ground beans into the kitchen. When I get there, the coffeemaker is gurgling and Dad is sitting in his robe at the table, reading the newspaper. He's got big sacks under his eyes.

"'Morning," I say.

His shoulders twitch. "Is it already?"

"Aren't you . . . late . . . for work?"

"I'm not feeling very well," he says.

"You . . . want some . . . toast?" I ask.

He doesn't answer. His face is buried in the sports section.

"You want . . . some toast?" I ask again.

When Dad looks up, I notice that his eyes are red and watery. His face is drawn, like a peach pit, and the skin on his neck looks worn out, like an old person. "Did you say something, Champ?"

I feel a lump gather in my throat and shake my head.

Dad goes back to his newspaper. I open the fridge and pull out the leftover Chinese food. I eat a few bites right out of the carton. It tastes like metal. I put it back and tell Dad that I'm going to the store to buy milk.

A foot of snow covers the roof like a clean sheet of paper. The early morning sky blushes, and the air is crisp and clear.

I climb the ladder and knock on the door to the water tower.

No response.

I unhook the latch and peer inside. Kiki is

curled in a ball, sound asleep. The wool blanket, pulled up tight to her chin, rises and falls in a steady motion. One boot pokes out the bottom, and I can see from an exposed sleeve that she didn't take off her jacket, either. Jupiter has snapped alert and lets out a low bark.

"Shhh . . ." Quietly, I lay down the paper bag containing a bagel and a small bottle of orange juice. I toss Jupiter a Milk-Bone. Then I leave Kiki to sleep in peace.

Mom is busy all day, tending to her patient, and Leo is out at a play date. A big pot of chicken soup simmers on the stove, and the kettle sings constantly. Dad has moved camp from the kitchen to the den, where the television hums and Mom flits in and out like a sparrow. When I grab my jacket and tell her I'm going to Flyer's, she says, "That's good, honey. No sense being cooped up in an infirmary on such a beautiful day."

157

★ ★ ★

I'm not sure what happens next: the sickness in my gut, the scream in my mouth, or the blood.

Kiki is sitting on the floor of the tower, hugging her knees and rocking. One pant leg is rolled up. A bloody razor blade lies on the floor between her and me.

The flashlight is on, and I can see two long thin wounds, like licorice whips, running down her shin. Above them is a fence of white scars.

The image swirls and blurs inside my head. I taste the Chinese food in my mouth.

It takes a minute for Kiki to notice me standing there. She snaps alert. Frantically, she pulls a wad of tissues from her pocket. She balls them up and blots the blood. "Could you leave me alone?" Her voice is low and calm.

I stand there stupidly, the way I stood in Zeke's doorway when we found him.

"Please," Kiki says.

A prickling sensation is working its way up the back of my neck. My face gets hot. I manage to get my boot on the razor blade without Kiki noticing. I drag it to the door and kick it out.

I don't remember climbing down to the roof, but when I do, suddenly I feel a throbbing at the back of my head. The world turns white. And then I throw up.

I stay crouched with my head between my knees until the dizziness goes away. My mouth tastes sour. My head aches. I walk around the roof and try to breathe.

What was Kiki doing? Should I go back up?

I keep walking. I drag my hand over the snow on the low concrete wall that rims the roof. I try to call up Charlie's horn to calm myself down.

The sky is a clear, cruel blue. Just like it was the morning we found Zeke. The thrashing voice in my head is just about to sink me into the memory when I hear a loud, harsh squeal.

*Keeee-keeee-keeee.*

I look up and see the hawk, perched on the tip of the tower. I swear it looks right back at me.

*Keeee-keeee-keeee,* it whines even louder.

I start climbing, hand over hand, on the cold metal wrungs. You'd think I'd scare the bird away as I get closer, but it just keeps crying its loud, haunting cry.

I push open the tower door.

My breath catches in my throat.

Jupiter is running in circles around Kiki. She is lying on the floor. Blood is spurting from her left arm like water from a hose. Beside her is the empty juice bottle, broken into a lethal shard.

I move closer. Her eyes are drifting back in her head.

My stomach rolls. My brain goes numb. "Kiki?"

Her mouth moves a little, but she doesn't answer.

I stand there for a minute, paralyzed. I watch the blood puddle around her arm. Suddenly, Jupiter jumps up and paws my thighs and barks. He snaps me alert.

I shake off my jacket and then my sweatshirt. I wrap the sweatshirt around the opening in Kiki's arm and tie it as tight as I can.

As I'm doing this, Kiki starts to talk. "It's all mine, Jed . . . it's my blood. I'm alive . . . my scars . . . they tell a story, my story . . . he can't take this away from me . . . no one can." Her voice is strained and halted. I can tell it is hard for her to breathe.

"Shhh," I say.

"I don't want to . . ." Kiki's voice fades out. Her mouth stops moving. Her eyes close.

My heart sinks into my gut. I touch the side of her neck. I feel the faintest throb of a pulse.

"You're not going to die . . . Kiki please . . ."

161

I slip my jacket back on over my T-shirt. Then, as fast as my legs will move, I race out the door and down the ladder.

Dad is reading one of his medical journals in the den. He peers over it. "Hello," he says wearily.

I open my mouth, but the words just fall all over one another.

Dad puts down the journal. His eyes grow wide with fear. "Joseph, what happened?"

I look at my hands and notice there's blood on them.

"Are you hurt?" He jumps up and moves toward me.

"This . . . girl . . . ," I manage.

"Yes?"

"She-she-she needs . . ."

"What's going on?!" He grabs my hands and examines them. He sees the blister on my left palm. "What is —"

"Can you?" I ask.

Dad is still trying to register what I'm saying. He puts a hand on my shoulder. "You're going to have to explain a bit better."

"Dad, *please!* I need . . . your help."

He nods.

"Can you . . . get your . . . coat? It's . . . an emergency."

A nervous look overtakes Dad's face. He follows me to the door. I open the hall closet, grab his down jacket, and hand it to him. He throws it on and slides his feet into a pair of boots. He looks down at his pajama bottoms. "Where are we going?"

"To . . . the roof."

"The roof! And what girl are you talking about, Joseph? What happened?"

I don't answer until we get in the elevator.

"She's . . . in trouble. . . . It's . . . bad."

A sharp crease forms between his brows.

"I'll . . . show you."

163

When we get to the top floor, Dad follows me up the stairs and out the door. "Where is she?" He sounds panicked.

I point with my chin to the water tower.

A look of alarm passes over his eyes.

"Are you . . . afraid . . . of heights?" I ask.

"Joseph, I don't know what you've gotten yourself into, but this better be —"

I take him by the arm and walk him through the snow to the base of the tower. I start climbing. I look back every few steps to make sure he is okay. I push open the door and, one by one, we step inside.

Kiki is curled in a ball. Her eyes are closed. Blood is leaking through the sweatshirt I tied around her arm. It's pooling on the floor around her. Jupiter is lying next to her, whimpering.

"What in God's name, Joseph?"

"She cut . . . herself, Dad. I think . . . she hit . . . an artery."

Dad rushes over. He feels Kiki's neck for a pulse. He gently lifts her good arm to feel her wrist as well. "What's her name?"

"Kiki."

"Kiki, can you hear me?" At the sound of his voice, she tries to move her head. A stream of drool trickles out of the corner of her mouth.

Dad unties the soaked sweatshirt from Kiki's arm. Then he shakes off his jacket, pulls off his pajama top, and ties a fresh tourniquet. He pulls his jacket back on over his bare chest.

"You're going to have to help me get her down the ladder. Do you think you can do that?"

I nod.

Slowly we get Kiki to her feet. Dad holds her under her armpit and wraps her good arm around his middle. I steady her on the other side. As smoothly as we can, we inch her toward the door. I hold Kiki and turn her around while Dad shimmies down the ladder a few steps. He takes the seat of her small body onto his shoulders, the way he sometimes carries Leo. It's my job to hold both of Kiki's hands in one of mine, to keep her from tipping backwards. It's a slow, scary trip down the ladder.

After Dad and Kiki finally reach the roof, I go back up and get Jupiter. Dad lifts Kiki off his shoulders and cradles her in both arms like a bundle of twigs. When I'm down, Kiki opens her mouth and tries to speak. "Poems." I think that's what she says.

"Shhh," Dad says. "Don't try to talk." Then he tells me to get his wallet. He says to bring the dog to Mom and tell her where we're going and that we'll call her from the hospital. He'll take Kiki to the lobby and wait for me.

"Should I . . . call an ambulance?"

"I can handle this. Just hurry!"

I follow Dad's instructions. A few minutes later, we hail a taxi.

I help Dad get Kiki inside, then race around to the other door and jump in.

"Take us to St. Vincent's emergency room," Dad says urgently.

He has Kiki on his lap with her legs folded between us. When we pause at a yellow light, Dad yells to the driver, "Sir, please! You're always driving like maniacs. Can't you now?"

The driver blows through the light and speeds across Eleventh Street.

Dad turns to me. He must see me shaking, because he doesn't ask me any more questions about Kiki. He just looks back and forth from me to her and says with quiet conviction, "We'll make it, buddy."

# NINETEEN

# "FLYING HOME"

As soon as we get to Dad's hospital, he rushes Kiki through the doors of the emergency room, with me following close behind.

"Help me, please!" Dad shouts.

A nurse comes and sees the blood leaking from Kiki's arm. "Follow me!" she tells Dad.

We sprint down a hallway to a small room at the end. Dad lays Kiki on the bed as nurses and techs race in and motion us to the back. There's an immediate rush of activity. Hands moving, voices volleying. I can see them stick an I.V. in Kiki's good arm and tons of other tubes all over her. They check her vital signs and blood pressure.

Dad falls into a chair. His chest is heaving.

A short woman enters the room. She has

shiny black hair pulled into a low ponytail and kind eyes shaped like olives. She walks over to Kiki and examines the wounds on her leg and arm. She checks the EKG, then instructs one of the nurses to get a urine sample and type O blood.

"Dr. Diamond?" she says, walking over to us.

"Dr. Chandra." Dad gets up from the chair.

"Do you know this girl?" Her voice is surprisingly calm.

Dad shakes his head and looks at me.

"Not really," I answer.

"Can you tell me what happened?"

"Joseph," Dad prompts.

"She cut . . . herself . . . with a razor . . . blade. And . . . broken glass."

"Is she on anything? Drugs? Alcohol?" Dr. Chandra asks.

"I don't know. . . . I don't think so."

Dr. Chandra nods. "The urine will tell us. Do you know how much blood she's lost?"

I look at Dad.

"Quite a bit, from what I can tell," he says. "Half a pint. Maybe more."

Dr. Chandra thanks us and dismisses us to the waiting room.

I'm feeling queasy. I ask Dad if we can go around the corner and get a Coke.

"We're staying right here, buddy. You can get something out of the vending machine. Sit down. I'll be right back."

Dad goes over to the pay phone and calls Mom. He lets her know that everything is okay. Before hanging up, I hear him say, "I'm about to find out."

Dad comes back with a can of Coke and a cup of coffee and sits down. "Do I need to ask questions, or are you just going to explain?"

I open the Coke and take a sip. I run a finger around the rim of the cold can.

"You might want to start by telling me who

this girl is," Dad says evenly. "Does she have parents we should call?"

I shake my head. "I-I . . . I."

Dad puts a hand on my shoulder.

"I have . . . this notebook. It belonged . . . to Zeke." I stare at the faded patches on my jeans. I brace myself for Dad to get up or tell me he doesn't want to talk about him. But he just squeezes my shoulder. He gives me a puzzled look, but says, "Go on."

"He wrote . . . all these poems . . . about New York. There was one . . . about that . . . girl. At least . . . I thought . . . it was her."

"What do you mean? Who is she?"

"I don't know. . . . She said she's traveling. . . . I don't think she has a family." The more I talk, the more the words loosen up in my mouth.

"Where did you meet her?"

"On the street."

"She's a homeless girl?"

171

I nod.

"And the water tower? How did you —? How long have you —? You could have killed yourself going up and down that ladder!"

I stare at my hands.

"Joseph, do you know what a risk you've taken? Why didn't you tell us?"

I nod again.

"What were you thinking?"

I don't know how to answer that.

"This isn't like lending a friend ten bucks. We're talking about taking someone's life into your hands. Do you have any idea how much responsibility that is?"

I nod.

"Do you really, Joseph?" Dad rubs his hands across his face and through his hair. He takes a deep breath and lets it out audibly.

"Wouldn't you . . . have helped her? If she asked you."

172

The question pulls Dad up short. "There are so many people on the street who need help. The problem is much bigger than you or I can solve by ourselves."

"So is affordable health care . . . but you still volunteer at the clinic."

Dad can't help but let loose a small smile. "But you have no idea what kind of baggage someone is carrying — if she's a drug addict, or has serious psychological troubles."

"She's not a drug addict."

"Okay, but still. You've got to be careful. This is New —"

"New York City." *No place to be careless.* "I know, Dad."

"I'm not sure you really know." Dad shakes his head. He leans over and cradles his face in his hands. His back goes up and down as he breathes.

"It made me . . . feel closer . . . to Zeke."

Dad lifts his face to look at me.

"Like somehow . . . we were in this together."
I shrug. "I guess that sounds . . . weird."

Dad reaches up to lay a hand on my head. He just keeps it there without saying anything.

A few minutes later, Dr. Chandra appears. "Well, it looks like no drugs or alcohol in her system. She punctured an artery. The wound is quite deep. But she's going to be okay. She's sleeping now."

"Oh, thank goodness." Dad takes Dr. Chandra's hand. "Thank you."

She grimaces. "She wouldn't say where she's from. We have no one to contact. Do you know anything?" Dr. Chandra looks at me.

"Her name . . . is Kiki. She's traveling right now . . . along the East Coast. She wants to be . . . a writer." I tell them what else she has said, how these scars were her story and no one could take that away from her.

They both shake their heads and frown.

"She seems like a sweet girl. She must have had it pretty rough." Dr. Chandra takes a breath. "I've seen gunshots, car accidents, knife wounds, you name it. But for some reason, the self-injurers really get to me."

Dad nods.

"Maybe we can talk about some options for her in a little while." Dr. Chandra smiles and starts to walk away. She turns back and looks at me. "I just remembered, before she fell asleep, she asked me to find out if you'd read the walls. I assume you know what she meant."

I nod, even though I don't.

Silence falls around us when Dr. Chandra leaves.

"Was Zeke trying . . . to hurt himself, Dad . . . trying to kill himself?"

Suddenly Dad looks like one of those watches where you can see the insides moving around. I see parts of him turning and grinding. In a soft voice, he says, "What makes you ask that?"

"He knew he shouldn't drink a lot. He knew he had to eat right after taking his insulin."

Dad takes a deep breath and lays a hand on my leg. "Zeke liked to walk the edge, but I don't think he meant to slip off it. Is that what you've been thinking?"

I shrug. I feel a hotness behind my eyes. "Sometimes."

Dad squeezes my thigh. "I don't think he wanted to die. Looking back, there weren't any signs. And your brother was a writer, remember?"

"What does that have to do . . . with anything?"

A pained look takes over Dad's face. He tries to smile through it. "He would have left us a note."

I feel an easing in my chest. Why hadn't I thought of that?

"Unfortunately," Dad continues, "a lot of

teenagers with diabetes tire of the shots and the daily self-testing. They think if they go off their insulin for a day and feel fine, that maybe they can live without it. Ezekiel was young. He liked to experiment. He thought he was invincible. Why do you think I was so hard on him?"

"I didn't know all that."

"Was I too hard on him?" Dad grimaces. "I'm not sure. I thought he needed a firm hand. I wish I could have done things differently." His voice fades. The muscles in his face clench and then collapse.

"You think about that, too?"

Dad takes a breath and nods. "All the time."

I stare down at the linoleum floor. "If I'd stayed home on the Fourth, he might still be here."

"No, Joseph. It's not your fault. Don't do that to yourself." He looks at me. He folds his lips inward till the shadow of his mustache and beard meet.

"What?"

Dad shakes his head. He pinches the bridge of his nose and inhales deeply like he's sucking back tears. We sit there in silence.

Does Dad think it's his fault that Zeke's gone? For the first time it hits me that maybe he feels responsible for not being able to save him. When I look at Dad, I notice that every part of him sags — his arms and his skin and his mouth — like he's buckling under the weight of something.

I know what that feels like.

"Part of me is relieved sometimes . . . that I don't have to worry about him anymore," I say. "I know that makes me a terrible person."

"I feel that way, too," Dad says quietly. "But it's only natural. We worried because we loved him. And it's the worry we're glad to be free of, not Zeke."

The weights on my limbs seem to drop off one by one. Could that be the answer? To let go of everything I'd been holding on to? To believe Dad?

178

"It's been a rough six months," he says. "It's been the roughest time of our lives. I thought losing my dad was the worst thing that could ever happen to me, but at least as I got older, I realized that in the natural order of things, it made sense. He was older. He was supposed to pass on before me. But losing a child —" Dad stops and shakes his head. "When you lose your spouse, you're called a widow or a widower. When you lose your parents, you're called an orphan. But there is no word in the English language for the loss of a child — or a brother, for that matter."

That almost sounded like Zeke talking.

"I feel like I lost a piece . . . of myself," I say. "Without Zeke . . . sometimes I don't know who to be."

"I know how you feel."

It's quiet for a minute after that. I can feel the space between us shrinking.

"How come you're never home?"

179

Dad rubs his eyes. He stares out into the lobby. A few people are reading magazines. The television hums.

"It's hard for me to face what's at home — what's missing from home."

"Not everything . . . is missing."

Dad's chest caves as if I'd poked him. He looks down at his hands. He sips his coffee. I sip my Coke. We watch people come and go through the hospital doors.

"I need you," I say.

Dad closes his eyes and nods. He puts an arm around me and rests his chin on my head. "I'm sorry, buddy. I'm so sorry."

Even though Kiki is still sleeping, Dr. Chandra lets me look in on her while she talks to Dad. "Don't wake her, though. She needs the rest very badly."

I leave them in the waiting room and walk down the hallway to where Kiki is. Her short hair fans out in a halo on the pillow. She's still got a million tubes in her and bandages on her left arm. The palm of her right hand is turned toward the ceiling. Her body is still.

I walk to the side of the bed. I gently touch her hair. It's soft, like Leo's after a bath. "You have to get healthy, Kiki," I whisper. "Dr. Chandra will take good care of you. And we'll look after Jupiter, don't worry."

Her chest goes up and down in a steady rhythm. She looks peaceful.

I reach inside my T-shirt and touch the *milagro* around my neck. I remember what Velly said when he gave it to me. *". . . You may feel grounded now and for a while. . . . But,* por favor, amigo, *don't forget your wings. . . ."*

I think he would understand.

I unhook the leather cord and place the *milagro* in Kiki's open hand. Then I gently close her fingers around it.

181

Her eyelids flutter. Her mouth twitches at the corners. Her eyes open halfway and then fall shut again. Her hand squeezes ever so slightly around the *milagro*.

I lean over the side of the bed. I let my lips brush her forehead. And then I say good-bye.

It's late when we leave the hospital. Dad and I grab a couple of slices of pizza and decide to walk home.

"Kiki's going to the psychiatric ward," Dad tells me, "as soon as she heals. Hopefully her doctors will be able to get more information about her, so they can decide what to do. She's still a minor, so if no one comes looking and she doesn't identify any family members, then she becomes a ward of the state. That could mean foster care or a group home or a psychiatric hospital. It depends how serious her illness is."

"Can I visit her?"

"In another few days, maybe a week. The doctors might want to give her a chance to acclimate. I'll find out."

I notice Dad dodge a pile of dog crap without even looking down at his feet. For some reason, that makes me smile.

At Fifth Avenue and Tenth Street, the DON'T WALK sign blinks and we cross the street.

"Am I in trouble?" I ask.

We continue east toward our neighborhood. We walk for several more blocks. Finally Dad says, "I haven't decided yet."

T
W
E
N
T
Y

# "THE LULLABY OF BIRDLAND"

On our first day back to school, Flyer waits for me on the steps of his building. He greets me with his Cheshire Cat grin. We knock fists. "Whazzup?" we chant at the same time.

"Nice locks," I say.

"You like it?" He rakes ring-studded fingers through his blue hair. He hops on his board. Ollies into the air and tail grabs the end. He lands then nollies into a sick heelflip. "That's the opening of my project," he says. "Velly told us to be original, right?"

"He's going to love it."

We glide up the street.

I think about the documentary, how I spent the rest of vacation working on it. Dad's the only one who's seen what I've done.

184

He came to talk to me the day after everything happened with Kiki. I was in my room hanging out with Jupiter.

"I want to make sure you understand the seriousness of what you did. And let you know that things are going to have to change around here." His voice was firm, but not scolding.

"I understand, Dad."

"Because Mom and I think you crossed a line . . ."

I could feel myself shrinking under his gaze.

". . . your actions these past few days have changed you. . . ."

I kept stroking Jupiter, waiting for the punishment to come down.

". . . you've matured so much." Dad's voice turned suddenly soft.

I looked up at him. "Aren't I in trouble?"

He looked back at me for a long time, collecting his words like shells on a beach. "What you did was really decent. Most people would never put themselves out to help someone. Especially someone they hardly know.

"Still, next time something serious comes up, we need to discuss it, beforehand." Dad bit his lip. His voice lowered. "I know it's been hard to talk . . . and, well, I don't want that anymore. I don't want to let you down. I'll be around more, buddy, okay, I give you my word on that. Will you give me yours that you'll talk to me? Man to man?"

"Man to man," I'd said.

"I love you all equally, you and Ezekiel and Leo. I'm sorry if it hasn't always felt that way.

"You've always been such a solid kid, grounded, smart, sensitive, reliable. Maybe Mom and I took advantage of that. We never meant to hurt you."

"I know, Dad." And for the first time, maybe ever, I really did feel that.

Then Dad leaned over and hugged me harder than I can ever remember.

"Hey, Jedi," Flyer pipes into my thoughts. "Want to go out West?"

"What do you mean?"

"I mean I'm flying out to San Francisco in April, to visit my mom. What did you think, I was running away?"

I shrug.

"Dude, get real. You need me too much." Flyer smirks. Then his face turns serious. "I guess it was stupid of me to think she was coming back. It's just that she and my dad always worked stuff out in the past." Flyer's voice cracks. He takes a breath and shakes his head. The sunlight catches his earrings and makes them shimmer. "Anyway, my dad's going to some ashram up in Sonoma while I spend a week with my mom. He wants me to join him for a couple of days before we come home."

"Cool."

"I don't know, man. A bunch of hippies sitting around chanting and twisting their bodies into ridiculously weird positions. Does that sound like a good time to you?"

I laugh.

"So maybe you could come. My dad said he'll talk to your parents if you want."

"I'll talk to them," I tell him.

He lands a soft, grateful punch on my arm. I mess his crazy blue hair. Then I race up the street, with Flyer skating as fast as he can to catch me.

When we get to class, Velly is all smiles. "*¡Bienvenidos, amigos!* Welcome back!" He opens his arms. He spreads his fingers. He tips his head to each of us. "*Cuánto los he echado de menos.* I've missed you."

People slowly settle into their seats. Velly asks all who've made a visual record of their neighborhood to please display it at the front of the room. Soon the ledge of the chalkboard is lined with paintings, collages, and photographs. There are images of Central Park, a memorial for the Twin Towers, two girls skipping rope on a sidewalk, old women sitting on stoops in folding chairs, housing projects that have been changed and brightened by the artist's hand.

One by one, we're asked to come to the front of the room and represent. In addition to the pictures on display, there are essays and stories, a scrapbook and an original song, and of course Flyer's righteous skating. Velly was right: Together, the visions of our different neighborhoods really do create a collage of the city.

I am the last one to get called. I go up to the front of the room, pull down the screen from the top of the chalkboard, and lower the lights.

Before I start the documentary, I take a deep breath and say steadily, "My record is of the East Village. It is a collaboration between me and my older brother, Zeke, who died from diabetes this past summer.

"Zeke was a poet," I continue. "He collected his writings on New York and probably would have gone on to become the next Walt Whitman or Langston Hughes." I turn on the laptop on a desk beside me. The screen at the front of the room becomes black. Slowly, white type emerges:

# BIRDLAND

A WALK-U-MENTARY IN WORDS AND PICTURES

THROUGH NEW YORK CITY'S EAST VILLAGE

ONE OF THE WORLD'S COOLEST NEIGHBORHOODS

BY JOSEPH DIAMOND

INSPIRED BY THE WRITINGS OF

EZEKIEL DIAMOND

The type fades out. The screen brightens. Jamal and his drum emerge. I drained all the color from the film, so the result is a grainy black and white, like Super 8.

In a smooth, unhalted voice-over, the whole class hears me read:

His hands are like Ping-Pong paddles
His voice is like wind chimes
Music pops and dips
He smiles
and sings
Handing out pieces
Of Himself
Like a deli owner
doling Halloween candy
To greedy and grateful children
Am I that generous?
Are you?

Jamal's hands fly over his drum, and behind him, in muted tones, you can just make out the subway platform. The people who walked through my shot are blurred, and I edited out the drunk guy completely.

191

The subway platform dissolves into the street, where deep grays swell to bright whites. Jamal's drum solo melts into Charlie Parker's "The Lullaby of Birdland."

The camera sails up Avenue A. As it collects images from Zeke's poems, Charlie's saxophone goes wild. Soon we are at the park, with the Queen and her dogs. After a few sound bites from her interview, the voice-over comes on again:

THE QUEEN OF CANINES

REIGNS

OVER HER RETAINERS

STEERING HER TEAM

A CHORUS OF YELPS AND MOANS

RISES DOGS STRAIN

AT THEIR LEASHES

EAGER AND JUBILANT.

The camera sweeps past Jesus, down Avenue B to the city garden. On a bench beside the sculpture sits my dad. He watches Leo inspect the animals near the bottom and then gets up to help Leo climb.

Slowly they fade into an image of Mom at her piano. A shaft of sunlight illuminates her face as her fingers sail over the keys like butterflies. The camera makes a brief tour of our apartment, ending with the open doorway to Zeke's room.

From there it cuts back to Avenue A and takes us inside the café to Melody. "The East Village is a wonderland," she says. "A waking dream, a mad tea party, a poem come to life." She turns toward the espresso machine, cranks the coffee in its socket, and winks.

Melody fades into an image of Kiki on the street, shaking coins in her cup as people, seen only from the waist down, pass by her and Jupiter. You can't really make out Kiki's face, but to me,

193

she is immediately recognizable. I've slowed down the motion speed, so the moment unfolds in half time.

The music falls away as I read:

THEY ARE BEAUTIFUL AND WORN
THEY ARE ANGRY AND SCARED
THEY ARE SOMEONE'S SISTER, BROTHER,
    DAUGHTER, FRIEND
DO YOU SEE THEM?
ONE GIRL IS LIKE A JACK-IN-THE-BOX
POPPING UP ON EVERY VILLAGE STREET
HER HARD-SOFT EYES HAUNT MY DREAMS
HELP ME HELP ME HELP ME
PLEASE.

Here Charlie's sax solo rises as the shot hones in on Kiki's eyes. I've blown the image way up so you can't see the details of her face, just two beautiful and sad gray eyes, and my reflection inside them.

It's been a week since Kiki's been in the hospital, a week since I've been taking care of Jupiter. The Queen (whose real name is Mary) will be coming by our apartment to walk him today while I'm at school and Mom's at work. And I'm going to visit Kiki this afternoon. I have to thank her for finding the poems.

When Dad and I went back to the water tower to clean up, I remembered the words Dr. Chandra had passed along to me from Kiki. I took the flashlight and held it up to the walls.

My heart made a little bounce in my chest. I moved closer to get a better look.

In pencil, scratched into the wood, were poems. And a picture of a bird.

I almost didn't believe it until I made my way around the circle and read ODE ON A WOODEN

WATER TOWER. When I sucked in a breath, Dad said, "What's up?"

I pointed to the poem. He read the words, but I could see he didn't get it.

I pulled Zeke's notebook out of my messenger bag. I turned to the page and held it out to Dad, along with the flashlight. "This was Zeke's book, Dad. I found it after he died. I should have shown you."

As Dad read the poem, his lips twitched and fluttered and finally curved into a smile. He turned back to the wall and then back again to the book. His mouth opened. "You think? Up here? Well, I guess it shouldn't surprise us."

In the documentary, Kiki's eyes dissolve into bicycle wheels, riding up the street. The wheels meld into a bright moon in a deepening sky, resting above our water tower.

The film tones grow smoky and the music softens as I read:

196

DARKNESS SPREADS

ITS GREAT WINGS

OVER THIS GREAT CITY

OVER STILL PLAYGROUNDS

AND HUSHED BUSINESSES

AND EMPTY SHELTERS

WHILE LAUGHTER SPILLS

FROM SAD CAFÉS

AND SIRENS CIRCLE

DOWN

AND DOWN

LIKE TEARS

IF YOU LISTEN

YOU CAN HEAR THE STREET ANGELS

SINGING SOFTLY

IN THE DEEP

BONNE NUIT, NEW YORK

BONNE NUIT.

The screen fades to black. From the darkness, perched on the crest of the water tower, the hawk emerges. Slowly, it spreads its great wings and, with broad, rowing strokes, lifts into the air. It wheels and circles in one long, graceful arc before disappearing into the deep unknown.

The screen fades to black. Final lines of white type appear.

IN MEMORY OF ZEKE "BIRD" DIAMOND
1985–2002
BONNE NUIT, ZEKE

THE END

ON BROAD, STRONG WINGS, I SEND HEARTFELT
GRATITUDE TO THOSE WHO HELPED THIS STORY
SOAR:

As ever, to my writing group, Anne Burt, Stephanie Carlson, Andrea Sheridan, and Ann Somerhausen, my first set of eyes.

To Billy Goda, who lit a fire under me.

To Jonathan Small, for his thoughtful comments as well as for his expertise on filmmaking and street slang.

To Melissa Caruso Scott, for creating such a memorable café and for entertaining me with tales of the city.

To Heidi Kilgras and Kimberly Williams, for accompanying me on the making of my first East Village documentary.

To Steve (whose last name I never learned), a Sixth Street and Avenue B Garden angel, who appeared seemingly from nowhere, let me into the garden after hours, and shared the story of its one-of-a-kind sculpture.

To Dr. Jorge Kizer, Carrie Mack, R.N., and Dr. Richard Riggins, for generously consulting with me on diabetes and medical procedure.

To Gideon Chase, skate master, for his thorough fact-checking of my skateboard terms.

To Gail Hochman, an agent in a million.

To Anne Dunn, my wise and compassionate editor, who lifts me up when I am grounded and always sends me flying.

To Leslie Budnick, for countless reasons, big and small.

To Liz Szabla and Jean Feiwel, for their faith in this book and for the precious gift of time.

To Marc Tauss, for his exquisite jacket photographs.

To Marijka Kostiw, for her beautiful design and for giving me my first *milagro*.

To Pam Conrad and Danny Pearl, dear friends and birds of paradise, who continue to influence me from the deep unknown.

To my grandmother Anne Caroline, whose enduring presence brings me deep comfort; and to my uncle Mickey Caroline, who was the first to notice her flying through our lives.

To Michael Citrin, the poetry and music in my life, for his brilliant mind, his sensitive insights, and his sparkling sense of humor, and for introducing me to the world of jazz. A novel's worth of thanks would never be enough to express all that he has given of himself to me and to this work. You are my *milagro*.

AND FINALLY, TO NEW YORK CITY — CAULDRON AND CRADLE TO THE CREATIVE SPIRIT — A MODEL OF STRENGTH AND MY DAILY INSPIRATION.